perfectly
dateless

perfectly
dateless

A Universally Misunderstood Novel

kristin billerbeck

Revell

a division of Baker Publishing Group
Grand Rapids, Michigan

© 2010 by Kristin Billerbeck

Published by Revell
a division of Baker Publishing Group
P.O. Box 6287, Grand Rapids, MI 49516-6287
www.revellbooks.com

Printed in the United States of America

Library of Congress Cataloging-in-Publication Data
Billerbeck, Kristin.
  Perfectly dateless : a universally misunderstood novel / Kristin Billerbeck.
      p.   cm.
  Summary: Entering her senior year at St. James Christian Academy, Daisy has less than 200 days to look stylish, develop social skills, find the right boy for the prom, and convince her parents to let her date.
  ISBN 978-0-8007-3439-8 (pbk.)
  [1. Dating (Social customs)—Fiction. 2. High schools—Fiction. 3. Schools—Fiction. 4. Christian life—Fiction.] I. Title.
PZ7.B4945Pe 2010
[Fic]—dc22   2010006048

Published in association with Yates & Yates, www.yates2.com.

10   11   12   13   14   15   16   7   6   5   4   3   2   1

This book is dedicated to my wonderful blog readers, who keep me young at heart, giggly, and inspired throughout what would be a lonely workday. Thanks for sharing your thoughts with me, both publicly and privately.

❦ 1 ❧

Prom Journal
Operation Prom Date
August 21
196 Days until Prom

They say the first step to recovery is admitting you have
a problem. So I guess I have a problem. I am a bit of a
perfectionist, and my life is anything but perfect. In fact,
it's pretty messed up. I mean, sure, if you look at my
grades, I appear good on paper. No question about that.
But perfectionism is a lonely island, and it sort of feels like
land is slipping further away.

I'm a Christian, so I know you can't actually be
perfect, but I sure have tried, as I believe every Christian
should. Make the most of the talents God gave you, right?
I love the feeling I get when there's a red "A" scrawled
across the top of my paper. Now that is a scarlet letter
I can get behind! But if I get 98 out of 100, I sort of

obsess about the two I got wrong. It's just the way my mind works, but I need to be worrying about important things, like why my clothes aren't cool.

Claire, my best friend, says I'm warped. Could be. I'm not saying it's right or anything to obsess, I'm only acknowledging that I do. I've seen "Intervention" on TV, so I'm well aware that admitting the problem means I'm totally on the way to recovery. Besides, Claire's parents are normal and rich, so what does she know?

See my problem? Being perfect—impossible. Being a perfect weirdo—something I'm closer to than I'd like to admit. Another excuse? I'm an only child. My parents thought, "Why screw up many children when we could make one perfect child?"

I'm sure that's where my deranged thinking comes from—always look to the parents, you know what I'm saying? My mom says the apple doesn't fall far from the tree, but I'm hopeful that their tree was on a hill and I'm rolling further away as I write. The thing is, kids like Heather Wells don't care if you're weird simply because your parents are weird. You're just weird. And dateless.

My mom says this perfection thing all started when I was a baby and couldn't handle being in a dirty diaper. Well, yeah! That's disgusting. I mean, how is that weird to want to remove myself from excrement? What am I missing? I would think that's instinctual.

8

In more recent years, I have never missed a day of school, not since the third grade when I had the chicken pox, thanks to Missy Miller's birthday party with the lopsided cake and lame "Rugrats" theme. I got her a collectible Barbie in this fabulous, silky red ball gown, complete with tiara, and all I got was the chicken pox. So wrong.

Anyway, it's not like my parents didn't have a part in my issues either, but I'll get to that later. Back to my life on paper and the reason I'm in my current predicament.

Straight A's throughout my entire junior high and high school career (except for driver's ed, and that was so not my fault). If you were on a college admission board, you would see me as the student you wanted at your school, right? I mean, I am like every thirty-five-year-old's dream teenager, but if you're seventeen like me and you're someone who resembles a hot vampire in a certain movie? You are not going to look my way for a date.

I'm a freak of nature physically too. Five foot ten, and not in a good Heidi Klum way. In a giraffe-like, knobby-kneed, hanging-gorilla-arms kind of way. At that point, you're thinking "mutant," not "romance."

My dad's lanky genes are totally to blame for this. If I weren't so tall, I could consider all those little guys who might think about me as a dating option for prom. But I can't exactly have them stand on a block for the picture, now can I?

Lanky.

Gawky.

Bony.

Giraffe-like.

If I did skinny well, they would call me graceful, lithe, gazelle-like, slender . . . but I don't do it well, and that's why the Abercrombie shirt with Claire's hand-me-down, padded bra underneath was the perfect look for me. (Claire apparently went through puberty, but I'm still waiting, which at seventeen is cause for alarm, or—around here with everyone's money—for a visit to the plastic surgeon's office. What is wrong with people? That has to be uncomfortable, right? Sleeping on two hard water balloons? But perhaps it's just me.)

Now add to this bony package a wardrobe of homemade, "conservative" clothes, and you have a better picture of my so-called perfect life. Being perfect on paper doesn't actually transfer to real life—as I start my senior year in high school, it's time to add some practical living skills to my accomplishments.

So why care now? While I was rewriting my "Symbolism in Hamlet" paper four times last year, other girls were giggling, squealing about Zac Efron movies, and generally making themselves matter to people around them. I think I'm irrelevant. And that can't be good. A perfectly pathetic social life is the antithesis of perfection in high school.

I've been so focused on college, it almost feels like I've never been to high school. I simply endured a series of tests and deadlines, but I can't remember much of anything. Sure, I know the Pythagorean theorem, but do I know how to apply false eyelashes or why the Jonas Brothers are popular? No.

I've never had a single date, and while my parents wouldn't let me date anyway (long, irritating story), I wrestle with the fact that I've never had the opportunity to say no. I've never broken a heart, I've never even registered on a guy's heartbeat. I've flatlined. BEEEEEP!

If I don't change my life now, I'll spend the rest of it like this: alone and invisible, never in the moment, always striving for the next big thing, forgetting what lies behind. I might become the first teenager with Alzheimer's. What if the only impact I've had on St. James Academy is the gummy bear I left in the school chapel as an experiment?

So no dates, unless you count my dad's purity talk over dinner at Hometown Buffet, and I so do not count that. Like I want my dad to talk about stuff like that anyway, and in public? Over fried chicken? Then he pulled out a ring, and people around us actually clapped. OMGSH! My purity on display as cause for applause. I could have died! I mean, what if they thought he was just some dirty old man proposing to his young girlfriend? Didn't my dad get that? That's a stupid question, of course he didn't. Unlike me, my dad lives in the moment, never a thought to the future or what might happen. So part of my diligent nature must be his fault. Am I right?

Don't get me wrong, I'm as committed to purity as my dad wants me to be, but I don't want to announce it publicly. Sheesh, hire out a billboard next time! Unlike Madonna or Sienna Miller, I don't want my sexuality, or lack thereof, up for public consumption. Call me crazy, but I think my dad makes way too big a deal over it, like it's his trophy on the mantel, announcing he's a great dad. Whatever.

I'm so glad my parents care and all that, but I guess I wouldn't mind if they cared a little less overtly. Parents have no shame. My dad couldn't even spring for a fancy dinner, and my ring is nothing more than sterling silver.

"I worried you'd lose a diamond," he said.

"Try me," I told him, and he just laughed. Like I was joking!

I should sign up for the convent now, except we're not Catholic, and the clothing . . . gag! I am not doing any job that requires headgear and nursing shoes.

"After all," Mom told me regarding purity and my future life as a homemaker, "don't think Cinderella sat

12

around after marriage. She had work to do. A castle to run."

Somehow I prefer to think of Cinderella as having people for those mundane tasks, but Mom ruined that too. Sort of like she ruins all the good things about being a girl: no makeup, no pedicures, homemade clothes. I'm a wreck, and what's worse? Up until now, I didn't even know I was a wreck!

Just so you know, I'm not asking to be head cheerleader or anything. I just want to exist in this petri dish that is St. James Christian Academy. I can adopt a live-in-the-moment attitude without turning into my parents. There's middle ground. I'm sure of it.

So welcome to my prom journal. It's totally pink with little flowers and frilly designs, really girly so I can summon my inner female power, which my mom tells me is completely Proverbs 31—the woman in the Bible who managed her household and sold purple things. I'm just hoping it makes me more socially acceptable. I'm looking for an "Aha!" moment, and if journaling helps me get there—a little further from the family tree—that's success.

My parents are what you'd call countercultural (read: weird). My dad is a classically trained musician and actor who makes his living delivering balloons and singing telegrams, with an occasional speaking gig thrown in. Money has never been a huge priority for him. My mother is content to believe we have plenty, and life is one big craft-ing fair for her. Our house looks like a Jo-Ann Fabrics, except it's much more chaotic and I do believe we have more in stock. Having bare feet around here is like asking for a tetanus shot.

My mom has the rosy cheeks of a sixteen-year-old and the fashion sense of a ninety-year-old. If there was a flo-ral pattern in 1970, my mother managed to capture it in oversized dresses that resemble upholstery. She's currently on a diet, which usually makes her unbearable, but this time? She's included exercise, and now she's all perky and buzzing with unnatural energy. I think I like the grumpy version better, but this one is losing weight, so I have a feeling the mom Energizer Bunny is here to stay.

Anyway, this journal is my own little secret. I'm channeling my inner Queen Esther. Sure, my mom can aim for the house manager in Proverbs 31, but I've got bigger plans. Queen Esther saved her people (her year of beauty treatments included!). Granted, Esther saved her people from death and I'm only going for social redemption, but a girl's gotta start somewhere.

"Daisy!" Mom yells.

"In here!" I shout back, shoving the prom journal under my pillow.

She appears in the doorway. "Do you know where your father's duck costume went?"

14

"I'm quacking up, Mom. Why would I have Dad's duck costume?"

She misses the bad pun. "He needs it for tomorrow. He's doing a marriage proposal as the goose who laid the golden egg. Isn't that darling?"

I roll my eyes. "Sure, as long as you're not the bride. Doesn't he need a goose costume, then?"

She lifts up her sewing kit. "I'm going to fix it."

"Mom, if some guy ever proposes to me wearing a duck suit, just shoot me, okay? You be the hunter."

"Goose suit. I have to paint the feet brown. Ducks have orange feet."

"I'll make this easy. Any bird, all right? If the guy dresses up in any animal costume whatsoever, or worse yet, hires someone else to do it? My answer is no. And some geese have orange feet, just so you know. Most, I think."

"How did I raise such a snob? It's sweet this man is doing something different. Anyone can get on his knees and pull out a ring."

"Then any guy *should* get on his knees. And I'm sure my father dressing up like fowl has something to do with my haughty behavior."

She shakes her sewing kit. "Have you seen the tea bags? I'm going to dye the suit."

Am I the mother here? "No, Mom, but I imagine they're in the kitchen." Although in my house, one never knows.

"You should watch your attitude, Daisy. Those costumes pay for your tuition. You can't afford to be snotty when your dad's sacrifice is for you."

I'm sorry. Did she just say "sacrifice"? "I haven't seen the duck suit. Will you shut my door? I want to get ready for school."

She shuts the door, but not without one of her weary sighs that tells me how ridiculous I am. It never occurs to them that fitting my father for a goose suit for a big marriage proposal contributes to my behavior. Do they expect me to be normal in this environment? Does a polar bear raise a cub and expect it to turn into a penguin? Isn't Mom the one who is always saying the apple doesn't fall far from the tree? I'm weird because that's what I know. Duh.

Prom Journal
September 6
(School and My New Life Start Tomorrow!)
180 Days until Prom

I've racked up $447 working in the last three weeks at Checks R Us—a check-printing company that is now 24 hours because of the bank closures. It's great because they think nothing of paying me extra for my time, and I can work on weekends and everything, which for an office job is pretty great.

I haven't even had time to think about my prom journal, but I'm finally back here as I get ready for the new school year and the new me. Wait, that's not entirely true, I have had time to obsess about the number of days left until prom. I wake up first thing in the morning, and that number pops into my head. It's always one day less than the day before.

So wrong. I am supposed to be thinking about being

a normal girl. I even practiced this thing in the mirror where I say, "Oh my gosh, I totally love that!" And I insert some insanely happening cultural reference that reflects the current conversation.

By the very fact that I think in numbers first and know how many days I have left to find a date, I know that statistically, my chances for finding a prom date are dropping, yet every morning I'm haunted by that number. I've been trying to get up early and giggle girlishly in the mirror, like the popular girls do. Right now it sounds a little horse-like, but it's getting better. I'm going to try it out on Claire and see if she notices anything weird.

Claire, my BFF since preschool, is currently going all emo scene on me, so I can't exactly tell her my life's goal is to go to prom. Which it's not, it's just my high school goal, my short-term goal. See? Totally living in the moment.

Claire's eyes would roll out of her head if she heard about this. She'd write some depressing poem about it and tell me how hopeless I am to express my pointless thoughts on paper, a valuable resource. "Green" was her last phase, but she found her Mustang convertible was more fun to drive than her parents' Prius, so that ended the environmental phase. You can't be green and drive a car that sucks gas into its powerful engine like a kid slurping an Icee after soccer practice.

Claire's the one wearing a studded dog collar and calling me hopeless. You see the irony here? I'm on my own, and if I find comfort in a frilly pink journal, so be it. Pink is life affirming.

Besides, what's the point of promised purity if my parents don't trust me to test it? My dad should realize the purity thing has to be my idea, and if I'm going to stand on my own in college, he needs to understand I can handle myself on a date now.

So I state it here for the record. I will go to my senior prom if it's the last thing I do. I will obtain the secret prize: the photograph that proves I was not a total nobody in high school and that I could get dates, I simply chose not to. (I'm straightening my shoulders as I write this!) I need proof that I had some semblance of a social life. Senior prom is the one event you have to go to. All those other years can be erased with the right prom moment.

Let's put it this way. I've seen my mother's memorabilia, where she's in a freakishly hideous hot pink minidress, clinging to some nerd. I don't want to pass on to my children that (1) I had no taste, (2) my date was one step away from my first cousin, and (3) Grandma went to her prom, but Mommy didn't. I mean, you might as well put the sofa on the front porch at that point.

I have 180 days to find the perfect dress (one that stands the test of time and doesn't look like Lady Gaga

18

in the year 2024), talk my mother into letting me get blonde highlights, and nab the perfect date to redeem my sad excuse of a social life from total oblivion. It won't be easy, but I am committed to stay the course.

For future reference, there are a few roadblocks to this plan.

1. Guys don't seem to know I exist (with the exception of the boys I tutor on the baseball team—and call me picky, but I was hoping for someone who could spell "prom").

2. My parents believe only in the concept of courting (naturally, because they're married), so dating is out of the question until I'm of marrying age. Prom hardly counts, though, right? God says the faith of a mustard seed can move mountains, and I have to believe it's true. Maybe my dad will stand next to the mountain and budge just a tiny bit.

3. I do not plan on "putting out" until my wedding night. Nor do I see someone buying me a meal and renting a tux/limo as cause for losing my purity. You want it? It will cost two karats and a platinum wedding. I do have God's standards. Duh. As Beyoncé says, if you like it, put a ring on it. And it BETTER have a diamond, know what I'm sayin'? And you'd better not be dressed like a duck!

Mom's calling. More later!

❧ 2 ❧

"Daisy?" my mom calls. I shove my prom journal under my pillow, grab a nearby book, and grin. Mom appears and leans against the doorway. I think she feels my guilt on her mom-frequency because she never comes in here unless I'm writing in that journal.

"Hi, Mom!" I say with too much enthusiasm.

"What are you up to?" she asks me. "You sound guilty." She thins her eyes.

"Me?" I laugh uneasily. "I'm not guilty. Did you lose more weight, Mom? You're looking really good."

"You think so? I haven't weighed in this week." She turns and shows me her new, skinnier self. She's fresh-faced and pretty, but she wants to dwell on none of that since it's vanity, and a sin. I beg her to read the book of Esther and see how beautiful they made the queen look before she went to her king. It's biblical, I tell her. Get thee to Talbots.

She just tells me I'm irreverent. That's her favorite word: irreverent. As in everything and anything that isn't her point of view of Scripture is irreverent.

A laundry basket on her hip, Mom is standing alongside David Beckham, a poster I placed strategically so that when

Mom comes in and nags me, I have my equivalent of the stress ball Claire's dad has on his desk. Mom thinks the poster is because I love soccer, which works for me.

"Where did you get this?" She sets the basket down and holds up a T-shirt.

Ack! Abercrombie and Fitch contraband! I must have left it in the laundry by accident. *Be cool. Be cool.* I casually look down at my book. "I got it at Goodwill when I went with Claire. Fifty cents, can you believe it?" My mom cannot pass up a bargain, so she has to appreciate my good shopping sense.

"You went to Goodwill? With Claire?" Her eyebrow bends in her are-you-lying way. "To shop?" Unsaid: *Are you expecting me to believe this?* Claire's clothes are all from the mall. She's had to work hard to get the emo look, until discovering vintage.

I shrug without meeting Mom's eyes. Eye contact would be very dangerous at this point. "Lots of kids do the vintage thing, but I can't get past the grossness of it. I mean, who knows where that thing has been? Right? But that T-shirt was barely worn. How could I resist?"

"You're avoiding the question. Why is Claire shopping at Goodwill?" Mom asks. This is our version of the standoff. What Mom wants is a thorough explanation, and heck if I know why my best friend thinks black is the new black. Naturally, I haven't mentioned the dark poetry or the part about the plastic spider rings plunged through her nose. Claire is kind enough to remove it all before crossing the Crispin threshold. She probably fears my mother would bring Pastor Gorman over, and quick.

"Why does Claire do anything, Mom?" When in doubt, change the subject.

"Are her parents all right financially? Maybe if—"

"Mom, her parents are fine financially." In case my mom hasn't noticed, Claire's parents drive a Beamer and a Lexus fake SUV. Their bedroom suite is the size of our entire house, and you can tell all of this from pulling into the expansive driveway on the hill. If my mom thinks the Webbers need help from the likes of us, in our decades-old Pontiac and fabric-strewn house, her compassion has softened her head.

"You know how she likes to change things up," I add.

Mom's eyes are slivers now. Nothing tests my mother's Pollyanna view of life like us talking about Claire. "You almost got me off track. Claire's latest phase doesn't explain this!" She holds up the shirt like it's dirty underpants—outstretched between her forefingers and thumbs.

I admit, I think about lying, telling her the shirt is Claire's, but my conscience gets the better of me. "Mom." I try to grab the shirt, but she clamps those innocent-looking fingers around the wad, and she's like a lobster on lockdown. She is not letting go. I try one more tug. "Seriously, Mom, you told me I couldn't buy at Abercrombie, and I haven't, but I paid for this with my own money. I hardly see why I can't wear it. It's a perfectly good shirt. If some rich kid is done with it, why shouldn't I have it?" I cross my arms, staring up at Saint Beckham for strength. "Abercrombie got absolutely no money from me."

"Daisy May Crispin, I've told you, God looks at the heart."

"So now he sees my heart through my cool new T-shirt that I purchased for a song. Maybe he gets to see an 'm' or a 'b' stretched over it, that's all. What do you think?"

"I think that's not funny. It's irreverent."

I flatten my lips. "I saw the shirt at Goodwill, and I bought it because it's still cute. I thought I could wash it in hot water and it would be as good as new."

Okay, really? Really I squealed in delight that some rich girl outgrew my very cool T-shirt and her own mother tossed it into the Goodwill bin—traitor! I ran through the store to show Claire, like when Veruca Salt finds the golden ticket. That's what I really did, but that's the kind of full disclosure that leads to nights alone in my room.

"There's nothing wrong with your clothes. I had the popular styles during high school, Daisy, and it only got me into trouble. I want things to be different for you. You're focused on your grades, and that's what's important."

"Is it too much to ask that I don't stick out like the poverty-stricken dweeb I am? I just wanted to have one shirt you didn't stitch together." Catching her horror, I add, "No offense."

"Poverty-stricken! Of all the—Daisy, your father works so hard to make this education possible for you. I would think that would be enough to make you grateful." Now, even when my mother nags, she does it so sweetly, in this encouraging Barney-the-dinosaur kind of voice, that it radiates guilt like a sunlamp. "If you want to call us poverty-stricken, I suggest you take a trip with the missions group from church. People have it so badly, sweetheart. Don't mock what we've been given."

"Um, just for the record? I tried to go to Guatemala with church. You wouldn't let me go, remember?"

"I don't think it's appropriate for boys and girls—"

"To build a church together and run Bible camps? Mom, guys are half the human race. I have to get along with them at some point."

"You're a teenager now. Hormones are raging and it's not the best time."

"For building churches?" I have overstepped my boundaries because Mom's lip is twitching. "I'm sorry. It's not that I don't appreciate all your hard work, I totally do, but I'm tired of standing out in homemade clothes and I wouldn't have stood out in Guatemala, so you should have sent me. That's where they send the T-shirts for losing teams. So if my shirt said, 'McCain wins!' I would be totally fine there." It's not a bad idea. Maybe I belong in a third-world country.

"I didn't have Christian parents, Daisy."

Cue the violins. She gives me her passive smile, the kind with no teeth involved. She might as well pat me on the head.

"You answer to a higher standard, and that's a good thing. While those kids use their clothes and their appearance to get by in life, you're learning to stand on your own two feet and make your inside matter. You'll thank me for these rules someday."

Do not roll eyes. Do not roll eyes. That will only make it worse. I look down and realize I'm the social equivalent of those prairie dresses on the FLDS ranch—an Easter-egg-colored frock—who looks like I worship the god of bad fashion choices. Which wouldn't be a big deal if I lived on the cultish ranch and all the other girls dressed exactly like me. I mean, maybe it is fashionable there, you know?

"I want to take one walk down St. James's hallway without being laughed at."

"If they laugh, that's their problem, Daisy. It's building character in you because you know that clothes don't define you."

24

"It may be their problem, Mom, but I'm the one they laugh at, and that never feels good. Your prom dress may be laughable now, but I'm sure it was cool back then, right?"

"You can buy your own clothes. No one's stopping you from that. I just want approval first, and I've given you a list of stores I don't want to support."

"Those are all the stores that are for my age group. Would you like me to head to Coldwater Creek and get me a sweater with autumn leaves on it?"

"The more you spend on fashion, the less time you have for what really matters. These girls are only transferring their own insecurities, and look at you, you're buying into it." She picks up the laundry basket. "They're not your friends."

As evidenced by their rampant use of epithets in my direction. *Thank you, Mom.* I have no idea why my mother sees this particular store as the devil incarnate (her words, not mine), but there it is. "I don't want to be their friends. I just want to fly under the radar and escape their wrath."

"So why don't you try talking to them?" She pulls her hair out of its cotton headband.

"About what, Mom?"

"All those facts you come up with. You remember everything like you're reading an encyclopedia. It's just amazing to me. Don't you think the other girls would find that fascinating?"

"Could be, but I think it would be fascinating like how people are fascinated by the freak at the circus you pay a dollar to see, not like, 'Wow, how did we miss Daisy? She should be popular!'"

"Now come on, that's an incredible skill what you do with numbers."

I have a skill with random number facts. I can remember everyone's phone number since kindergarten. If I call for a pizza? That number is with me for life.

"I don't have room for the stuff these girls care about. So can't we compromise, Mom, and say the T-shirt can stay?"

"Wearing a tight T-shirt with the name of a store famous for erotic advertising is not the message I want my daughter sending to boys."

"Boys don't even know I exist. The chance of one of them being overcome with passion from my T-shirt? Very slim." I hold my thumb and forefinger together.

"This discussion is over." She puts her hand on the doorknob.

"Seriously, Mom, I could walk down the hall naked and I'd be lucky if I garnered a stare, so what's the big deal about a T-shirt?"

Mom's cheek twitches, and she looks like she's about to have kittens over my visual. Seriously, Claire wears a nose spider, and do you think anyone will look at her? We're totally invisible. They might as well park our desks under the bleachers, but in my mom's world, we're having to beat the boys away with a baseball bat. Don't get me wrong, I love that she thinks I'm so valuable, but I wish her view lined up a little better with reality.

I exhale as I watch my new favorite shirt muzzled into the laundry basket. All my hopes of looking semi-normal this year are wadded up with it. "But can we at least talk about my clothes?"

"There's nothing wrong with your clothes."

"I mean, can we talk about my clothes in the realm of the world's reality and not yours?"

26

"The economy is finally catching up to the way your frugal father and I have lived our lives. You're ahead of the curve, Daisy. I'll bet some of the kids you went to school with last year won't be there this year because of all those Mercedes and Land Rovers. If they had lived like your father and me . . ."

I've tuned out. I love my parents, but as much as the other parents bury themselves in the pride of their fancy cars and giant houses, mine bury themselves in the pride that they're above all that. They'd live "poor" no matter what they had—like there's never enough to go around. Nothing is given freely. Even the worst-worn blanket from the closet is given to the Salvation Army as if it's a prized treasure. Is there anything worse than the guy at the Salvation Army giving you a dirty look for your donation? If there is, I do not want to know about it.

"Are you giving boys some sort of idea?" Her eyes get round. "Because any girl can get attention if she's willing to give a boy ideas."

I hate to admit if I knew *how* to give a boy an idea, I might have tried it. Once anyway. "Mom, I just want to wear a pair of jeans to school."

"Christians aren't of this world, Daisy. We're not supposed to fit in easily. If other Christian parents choose to put their children's clothes in front of their morals, that's their business, but as for me and my house—"

"We will serve the Lord," I finish for her, throwing myself backward on the bed. "I don't see why we can't serve him in jeans. All I'm saying."

This is sort of my pet peeve. My mother makes us total freaks of nature, with her homemade clothes and hand-woven purses (and not the cool kind!), then says we're being punished for our faith. No, um, people in China are being punished for their faith. People in the Middle East are being punished for their faith. We're just reaping the rewards of being defiantly bad about fashion. Hello? The last time I checked, being called "nerd girl" wasn't spiritual warfare, just your standard high school misery.

"You're the one who chooses to spend your money saving for a car. No one is stopping you from shopping."

Okay, I beg to differ.

"Besides," my mom continues, "you look so cute in the clothes I make you."

"And Daddy looks cute as a goose, but that's hardly the point."

My mom sits beside me and pats my knee. Sometimes I think she grew up with too many of those old shows where the parents doled out wisdom like floss at the dentist. "Now is the time to focus on your future, not what other kids think."

Ugh. I am getting nowhere. Why do I waste my breath? "You want me to go to school looking like a total dork, don't you? It would make you happy if I never had a date!"

"Daisy." Her voice softens, and she puts her arm around me.

Here we go. The I-was-your-age-once spiel.

"Dating is for couples who are ready to marry. What would be the point of dating while you're trying to get into college?"

"Um, a social life? Because the male gender is half the school's population? Mom, I've never given you reason to distrust me. Can't you step out on a limb and let go of the leash a little bit?"

She holds up the shirt again.

28

"Besides that, I've never given you a reason not to trust me."

"It's not you I don't trust. It's the boys, and your father will confirm that if you have any questions there. You and Claire don't seem to be suffering any. Did I ever get to play tennis and swim at a country club all summer?"

"No, but I bet your dad never showed up to your 'Back to School Night' dressed as Batman either."

"Your friends loved that! They all wished their father could be so creative. You're not exactly suffering, Daisy. I think it's not too much to ask that you focus on what school is for and leave courtship for later."

"Mom, I am suffering. Okay, maybe *suffering* is too strong of a word, but I've been going to school with most of these kids my entire life, and they don't even know my name! I've become completely invisible and irrelevant." Not irreverent, irrelevant.

"So say hello and introduce yourself. That's not too hard, is it?" She balls up her fist and plops it on her hip in that "you are so ignorant" way. "Would you feel better if they thought your name was Abercrombie?"

"Abercrombie is a better name than Daisy Crispin. I sound like a breakfast cereal."

"You're far too worried about what people think, Daisy. You have a beautiful name." She squeezes my chin. "And a beautiful face, and one day when you don't have anything to look back on to regret, you'll thank me. On your wedding night—"

"No!" I clamp my eyes shut. "No, we're not going there!"

She laughs at me. "All right."

"Mom, look, I understand how you and Dad feel about dating, but it's my senior prom this year. I'm planning to go with my friends, and you can't expect me to go without a date. I don't even think they let you do that. Promise me that you and Dad will at least have this conversation, all right?" I flutter my eyelashes in my most innocent expression.

"Your father said this day was coming." She drops her head as if I've just told her I'm with child. "A boy called here yesterday, and I tried to tell your father it meant nothing, but he's proved me wrong yet again."

"A boy?" I try not to sound too interested. "I'm sure someone is only selling senior candy or the like."

"It was Chase. I realize you've been friends for years, but I don't think it's appropriate for Chase to call you now as you get older. I tried to explain courting to him, but he acted flustered, said goodbye, and hung up. Maybe a teacher should explain it to him. I may have overstepped my bounds. It's not my place to lecture him if his parents aren't up on the concept of courtship."

Yeah, a lecture on courtship. That's going to happen.

"Mom, please. Please don't make me any more of a freak than I already am. You know Chase; we've known his family since kindergarten. Wouldn't you rather I test-drive dating while I'm here rather than off at college when I don't have to come home at night?"

"Daisy! I'd rather you not test-drive anything. I don't like your metaphor at all. Life is hard enough as it is. Just focus on what you do well, which is school. The dating will come when it's time. Besides, kids today don't dance, they grind."

My eyes bug. "What did you say?"

"You heard me."

"I won't grind at the dance. Gross." I like my mother better when she's ignorant. It's less taxing. "Mom, I am the only girl I know who is not allowed to date at seventeen."

"I find that hard to believe. Surely there are other parents at St. James who feel the same way we do."

"I'm the only girl without a cell phone and the only girl who dresses like a hostess at Denny's."

"You're also the only one whose mother cares enough to sew for her. If everyone jumped off the Golden Gate Bridge—"

"I get it, Mom." I cross my feet at the ankles. This is pointless. She really leaves me no choice, because I am not going to college without that prom photo. And I am not using my Photoshop skills to get it. "So what did Chase want?"

"I told him directly that you don't take phone calls from gentleman callers and he hung up on me, so I have no idea, but I should speak with his mother about her son's phone skills."

"Mom! It's Chase from kindergarten! You're going to pretend you don't know who he is?"

"I know who he is, and when he was in kindergarten, a playdate was one thing, but now you two are older and there are repercussions to gentleman callers." She puts her fist on her chin.

"Gentleman callers! Mom, I don't live in your Jane Austen novels, all right? He probably just wanted to know if we had any classes together so we could exchange homework information."

Mom ignores my rational, plausible response. Come to think of it, my mom has one of those antique chaperone couches for three in the living room. That is not a good sign. I see my future with my dad between Chase and me on that sofa, and I am mortified.

31

"So you might want to explain to Chase when you get back to school about the courtship process." She taps her foot, annoyed I'm not listening.

I bang the back of my head on the wall in a steady rhythm. Explain courtship to Chase? I'd rather explain YouTube to my mother.

"Mom, Chase *has* to call me because he can't text me. I am the only human being at St. James Academy without a cell phone! I probably won't be able to get a job because my thumbs won't operate any equipment properly, having never learned how to text. People will think I don't have opposable thumbs."

"Spare me the drama, Daisy. We decided as a family that cell phones were a waste of money."

As a family, she means my dad and her. She distinctly left out a prominent member—and incidentally, the only one who wants a cell phone! She's already gone, though, taking her affixed laundry basket with her.

In my mother's defense (if she has one), she and my dad both had pretty wild backgrounds. The kind of stuff you don't want to think about in terms of parents, and I'm happy not to hear about it. My dad went to juvy for smoking pot in the school bathroom, and my mom did some things with boys she doesn't want to mention. Gah! If having my fingers in my ears while I hum is any indication, I don't want to hear it either!

Anyhoo, they feel they didn't get enough guidance as kids, so they've put me on one of those underwater tracks, guiding my every movement so I won't make the same mistakes. Honestly, I think if they could pipe in "It's a Small World" and shield me from the sounds of life, they would. I wonder

32

if they have any idea how lonely it is being perfect? And once you've tried, you know you can't be perfect, you can only pretend. I'm tired of pretending. I just want to be a little normal.

My half-thought comes out of my mouth. "I'm not perfect, I just play it at home."

"What did you say?" My mom reappears in the hallway.

"I said I'm all set for school. My backpack is perfect."

I lean back with my hands behind my head. Chase Doogle called me! And I can live for an entire week on that alone. What else is there?

❧ 3 ❧

With my mom gone from the room, I realize that school starts tomorrow, and I have yet to put anything important in my prom journal—meaning, the point of it, so here goes. The facts . . .

Prom Journal
September 6

Despite my mother's adamant protests, I have five possibilities for the perfect, photogenic date—six if you count a brooding Robert Pattinson (a girl can dream, can't she?).

Five is my favorite number, plus it's a prime number and a positive integer. I don't know why that brings me peace, but it does.

I read this article called "Boy Catcher's Eyes," and you know, it is probably written by someone like my mother, because who calls a guy a boy? But I'll practice it on someone who's not a real option at first. Then I'll go for the big guns later. I'm supposed to let him know I'm interested in him with my eyes. Sort of the way a lion-ess would devour a gazelle with her eyes before making a move, but without the teeth. I practiced in the mirror and it simply looks like I've lost a contact, but I'm totally working on it, and with a little practice, who knows who I might attract?

Back to my options for the ultimate prom photo:

1. Brian Logan
2. Steve Crisco
3. Greg Connolly
4. Kelvin Matthews
5. Chase Doogle

I'm starting with Brian Logan because he's probably the longest shot, and if he drops off early, that's only to be expected. He's super popular, which means in addition to not knowing I exist, getting on his radar is that much more difficult because he's always surrounded by throngs of hangers-on—people with names.

So Brian hangs around with the cool kids, he drives his mom's old Volvo convertible (sexy and yet oh-so-safe—my dad has to approve!), and he goes to my church, so my parents know his, though they won't admit to this if the time comes. He's probably out of my league, but I have to aim high, am I right? I mean, do I want to enroll in community college before trying for Stanford? So Brian's on the list, which I think says a lot for my optimistic view of my senior year.

Steve Crisco. He's on-fire hot, but not the sharpest knife in the drawer. His life's goal is to surf for Jesus. I'm not exactly sure how you do that, but he probably doesn't have the intellect to figure it out anyway, and his lifetime goals are not my worry. This is about the here and now, living in the present. I'm not getting married or anything. But like I said, he's a definite prom possibility—he's fun and the life of the party, so I'd be with the "in" crowd that night.

Steve cheated off me in Geometry, which is totally not okay, but I know he at least knows my name. In fact, I'm surprised he hasn't written it down on his test once or twice by accident.

Greg Connolly. I've known him since kindergarten, and he's more like a brother than a date possibility, and he's sort of reserved for when I get really desperate. He's the bench warmer of prom dates. Incidentally, he may not have had a date before either, but he can probably tell you any random fact about space movies. He's sort of the male version of me, which explains why he's not at the top of my list. If I wanted to date myself, that would be wrong on so many levels. With Greg, our limo might look like the bar scene in Star Wars because his friends tend to be as strange as mine, just on a more science-fiction level.

Greg has grown up to look like Orlando Bloom, and unless he made the Spock sign in the photo, he'd look great in the picture. He hasn't been marred by figuring out that he looks like Orlando. Zero self-confidence. So he's my secret weapon to pull out when it looks bleak, but of course, it's not going to look bleak because I, Daisy Crispin, have a plan. And you know, even if he doesn't open his mouth at all that night, or dance with me, he'll look smokin' in the picture. Besides, if the conversation gets thin, we can share math facts or talk about our PSAT scores.

Kelvin Matthews. Number four on my list keeps to himself, with his head to the ground and somewhere to be at all times. He's the shy, silent type and doesn't say much to anyone, but he knows my name and will smile if I call out to him. At this point, that's cause for hope. He's clean-cut, probably the best-dressed guy in school, and would look steamy in a photo, but the downside? He has better hair than me. I don't know, his nickname is Kel, but I want to call him Gel because his hands look like a jellied Halloween mask. So weird. But he's cute. And coiffed.

I suppose a journal to find the perfect date for prom is kind of perfectionistic and future-oriented, which I'm supposed to be working through, but if I don't record what I do wrong and what I do right, how will I get a date by next March? It's not like I have any record to go on here. And let's not forget, I still have to talk my parents into letting this happen, but I have nearly six months to move this mountain. The entire world could change in that amount of time—how hard could a simple date be?

The other reason I can justify a prom journal is that I felt it was wrong to put this in my prayer journal. I mean, sure, God knows how pathetic I am on my quest for high school meaning, but I didn't want to tempt fate by writing out real prayers for sick church members and soldiers in Iraq next to Chase Doogle's school schedule so I might stalk him a bit. I know that's probably all wrong biblically. God's not a Magic 8-Ball and he's on to me.

Claire isn't going to be any help in what I'm sure she must think is a ridiculous goal. She's currently sporting painted-on skinny jeans and straight, funky black hair over her one eye. (I preferred the green lectures she gave me on refraining from flushing the toilet so often, since being an environmentalist was her last phase.) Now, Claire is all negative about everything—and I've told her she needs to put on some pink (life giving) and be happy again, but she proceeds to recite dark poetry about how God's work on earth is serious business and to recite statistics on Darfur.

My mom thinks Claire might have a demon (Mom hasn't seen the worst of it), so she's praying all over the house whenever Claire enters. Which I find highly ironic, since Claire is always praying for my mother to see the severity in the world and stop buzzing around like a hummingbird. The truth is probably somewhere in the middle, but since kindergarten, Claire has drifted toward the latest trends, taken on the newest causes, and prides herself on being completely aware of the global plight of the world.

Claire tries to get her parents' attention, is all, and their dinner conversation tends toward what's current in the world. Their social calendar doesn't make room for Claire, so she makes herself known any way she can by being able to discuss hedge funds. You'd think Claire's parents would get a clue and pay attention to her, but no. They sign themselves up for one more funniest video moment after another in ignoring their daughter. She simply ups the stakes until they have no choice but to turn her way.

Emo is so yesterday anyway, which is out of character for Claire, so I know she's doing it only to annoy her mother and get a rise out of people. She'll be on to the next thing soon enough. All I can do is wait it out. She waited out my "High School Musical" fetish. I owe her.

Did I mention that Claire does not have the capacity to get embarrassed? I think she's actually missing that gene, so if Claire found out about my prom journal? She'd have no problem whatsoever humiliating me into dropping such a stupid quest, and she'd find me a date in her own way. She'd make it happen, no doubt, but at a cost I'm not willing to pay.

We go to a Christian high school, but a lot of the kids

who go there are just wealthy, not Christian. I read in "Time" at the dentist's office that the San Francisco Bay Area is the narcissist capital of the world. If I were judging by some of my classmates, I'd have to agree. Like my mom says, the apple doesn't fall far from the tree. Oh wait. Yes it does. Or I am absolutely without a prayer.

So the rich parents send their kids to a Christian school to keep them out of trouble (which doesn't work, but you have to applaud the effort). Claire's not like that, though. She's rich, but she loves Jesus—it says so in henna on her arm right now. She will be much less emo when school starts and she has to pass the dress code, which specifi-cally forbids the tattooing of oneself, even if it's tempo-rary. Thank goodness, because I'm not sure how much depression-as-an-act I can take. Seriously!

Claire's parents belong to the country club, where she summers. Okay, I'm with her sometimes, and I am not ready to abandon free Cokes, brought to me by a pool boy dressed in a uniform, because Claire is going through an identity crisis. I mean, dress like death and all, but can you get a black bikini and move on? I need a tan! If any-one should be emo, it's totally me. For obvious reasons.

But back to my prom date list and the frosting on the cake: Chase Doogle!!

I know his name is beyond bad. What were his parents thinking? You've got the whole cool "Chase" thing, and it's

40

such an obvious juxtaposition with "Doogle." They should have named him Dane or Daniel.

Can you imagine if I married him? Daisy Doogle. So wrong. It's not bad enough I'm named after the world's cheapest flower—practically a weed! But now, you combine it with my dream date's last name, and I can't even practice writing it without bursting into laughter. Daisy Doogle. Daisy Doogle. Daisy Doogle. It never sounds like anything but a Saturday morning cartoon.

Chase . . . sorry, I got lost there for a minute. The first time I saw Chase in kindergarten, my stomach went all Jell-O on me. He held my hand then, and stole a kiss at lunch by the big tree. (He got in big trouble for that one, but I like to think I was worth it.)

I can look into Chase's eyes and it makes me feel tingly every time. It's as though he's got this electromagnetic field around him, and when he comes close, I feel the buzz. In a way, I'm afraid to write his name down here, because I know it involves disappointment and I get into that jinx thing again. I don't deal well with rejection, especially by the one option who matters.

Chase Doogle is hotly photogenic, with his Adam Brody curls and his intense hazel eyes (sometimes more green, sometimes more brown—he's like his own mood ring). He's got this smile that is infectious and a laugh that makes everyone within range smile—just that special magic that exhilarates if he looks at you. But what makes him the pinnacle of all prom dates is that he's brilliant on top of that inexplicable charm. And dang, if I don't love a nerdalicious guy.

I wouldn't have to make the photo look perfect. It would be perfect.

Let the games begin.

❧ 4 ❧

September 7
First Day of School
Fact: $6.6 billion was spent on back-to-school clothes. None of it came from my house.

St. James Christian Academy is an enormous, private high school, set atop a hill on fifty sprawling acres in Northern California. If I were reading the brochure, its selling points would be that it boasts two Olympic-sized swimming pools, a dance studio, a full gymnasium, and world-class academics. It also has 2,000 students, 1,995 of whom have no idea who I am.

SJCA has that white-washed, clean concrete that shocks the eyes without sunglasses. It's like Disneyland without the fun. In fact, if you're caught littering, scraping the gum off the sidewalk is your punishment. The school emphasizes academics and intellectual pursuits but also offers a full athletic program, making jocks and cheerleaders a necessary evil.

I would say the campus is more intellectual than Christian, though all of the teachers are believers, and we have chapel every morning. The students themselves tend to come from four categories: (1) geeks on the fast track to a prestigious college; (2) uppity, rich slackers, whose parents are more hopeful than mindful; (3) athletes looking for that hard-won scholarship; and (4) students like me—sheltered Christian kids whose parents have sacrificed everything for the outlandish tuition so that the world cannot inflict itself upon us. You can tell my lot by our ratty, sturdy backpacks (not new every year), our cheap gym shoes, and our all-around inability to fit in.

k ■ k

I slog up the long staircase, behind all the glistening new backpacks and store-punctured jeans. Scanning the main courtyard, I see that Claire isn't waiting for me, and my heart completely drops. Momentarily I wonder if she met new friends and will be creating dark haikus at lunch without me. What if she's suddenly grown the humiliation gene?

Before I have time to panic, I hear her voice. "Oh my gosh, where have you been?" Claire sidles up to me and puts her mouth next to my ear. "So I was outside Mr. Walker's office getting out of Calculus this semester, like I need that kind of stress, and Amber was in there. She got sent out of zero period for having too much Amber, not enough clothing. Her mother had to come and bring her a shirt!" Claire, whose hair has magically turned brown for school and the dress code, shakes her head. "I cannot believe you missed it. With all she's said about your clothing, I would have loved for you to have been there. I wanted to tell Mr. Walker he should have seen her at the club in her bikinis this summer—they couldn't send her home from there."

"Didn't her father come bail her out?"

Claire raises her brows. "Daddy's in Washington."

We shouldn't rejoice in other people's misery. We under-

44

stand that, but Amber Richardson has picked on us since the day she first saw us in preschool Bible class at church. She came up and pulled a chair out from under Claire and then laughed, pointing at her on the ground. I helped Claire back up, but even as a preschooler, Claire wasn't going to take that garbage. She got up and pushed Amber to the ground with full force.

Of course Claire got in trouble, but we smiled at one another that Sunday morning, and a pact was made. We've been friends ever since. It was a fluke Claire was even there that morning too. Her parents needed to finish some project and dropped her off at church, having heard that parents didn't need to be there. Free Sunday babysitting!

"Amber hasn't changed a bit," I say. "She always needed too much attention. Remember her pulling up her lacy baby-doll dress so Matt Gimler could see her fancy panties in kindergarten?" Truth be told, I wanted those panties, and I wouldn't have shown them to any boys!

"Amber never gets caught, and when she does, her senator daddy just pulls out the wallet and everything goes away—but not today. I can't believe you missed it. You're always early, what happened?"

"Look at me," I say.

Claire looks horrified as she peers at me. The shock and awe on her face cannot be masked. She pulls me by my arm to the nearby bathroom. "You have the hugest zit I've ever seen."

I cover my face. "That's why I'm late! Thank you for confirming my worst fears, by the way. I tried to tell my mother I needed to stay home, or at least get her concealer, but do you think she'd let me? She said it wasn't that bad."

Claire pushes me toward the fake, unbreakable mirror and whips out a compact. "What are you thinking? Come on, there's listening to your parents, and there's this. There is no excuse for this."

I feel my forehead and the third eye I've grown overnight. "My mother said it wasn't that bad, and right now I'm inclined to believe her, because what else can I do about it?"

"Girl, your mama lies! Mt. Vesuvius looked less like it was about to blow than your forehead. That is disgusting!"

"Don't hold back for my sake, Claire," I say. "Mom wouldn't let me put makeup on it. She always says it makes things worse because it'll clog your pores. You're not making me feel any better about it." My confidence is waning. "This was supposed to be my senior year. A thrill ride, you know?"

"I'm not going to lie to you like your mother. I'd take the chance on clogged pores if I were you." She digs through her purse, pulls out a black tube, squeezes some of its liquid onto a sponge, and pounds it on my forehead. "Listen," she says as she rubs my face with vigor, "I'm not one to care about my appearance, but let's get real. We have to be considerate of others." She starts digging through her bag again, then she looks right at me, and I know I'm about to get a good dose of Claire-truth—which is not for the faint of heart.

"Don't say it."

"Say what?"

"Whatever it is you're thinking. I don't think I can take it this morning."

"I think you should turn your mother in for child cruelty. 'Not that bad,'" she repeats, clucking her tongue. "Your mother needs to look up once in a while from her needlepoint. How could she send her daughter off looking like this?"

I could mention that Claire's mother sends her off every day, but I don't.

Claire pulls out a small black box from her mother's hand-me-down Coach (still from the current season, she tells me). "I knew I had two in here. This is Amazing Base. Drew Barrymore swears by it, and this is my gift to you, and the entire school if I'm honest." She hands it over with all the fanfare of a religious sacrament. "Don't leave home without it, and quit stressing. You always break out when you stress. You'll get perfect grades again this year."

"It's not the grades I'm worried about," I tell her. I come close to spilling my secret, but I swallow it back down. "How much does Amazing Base cost?"

She raises her eyebrows. "What would that possibly matter on a day like today?"

"Good point." All my optimism for the new me has evaporated, and I'm afraid to leave the bathroom. Claire doesn't get embarrassed? She's embarrassed for me, and if that doesn't fill me with a deep-seated fear of rejection, I don't know what might.

"Your mom really doesn't want any guys near you. I mean, there's listening to your parents, Daisy, and there's committing social suicide. Like we need any help in that arena. Does she know that we're invisible? Did you tell her I brought a bullhorn to school last year and still no one listened to me?"

"She knows. She likes it that way." I rub the spot, which now looks like a simple deformity in my forehead since the concealer.

"Quit touching it!"

Even in the fake mirror, I can see that I look better. Presentable. Not hideous. "Thank you," I mutter, but my zeal for the new Daisy is gone. My feet are planted firmly in place, and I'm wondering what it would be like to cut my very first class of senior year.

"Come on, we'll be late!" Claire grabs me by the shoulders and yanks me out of the bathroom.

I'm pulled into the current of kids, all dressed in their new school clothes and shiny backpacks, and I want to retreat. It was one thing when all I had to do was get good grades, but suddenly I'm aware of how strange that is, how strange I am. I think it's how Adam and Eve must have felt after eating that fruit.

"I was stupid to think I could do this. I'm a good student." That's it. That's enough.

I cuddle my backpack close to me. Claire, though she has no idea what I'm talking about, has crumpled her forehead in concern.

"Daisy, you said you were going to stand up to her this year. I do believe 'This year is going to be different' were your exact words. Yet, here you are, ready to hostess at Denny's."

I look down at my white ruffle blouse and my black pants and beg for mercy. "Claire. Please don't."

"Denny's, Denny's, Denny's."

"You could grow a little so I could wear your clothes, shorty. That would be the friendly thing to do. Make your dad get you some of that growth hormone at the plastic surgeon's office he talks about."

"He talks about that because he's suing one of them for appendages growing that shouldn't. No one wants the arms of a gorilla. I certainly don't, so you're going to have to come up with a different plan."

I shrug. "I'd only want the clothes your mom buys you

anyway. Not the ones you pick out yourself. Cute outfit, by the way." I run my finger up and down at her. She's wearing this darling little summer tunic dress in a bright turquoise with a purple sash around it. "Does this mean emo is over?"

"I wasn't emo." She rolls her eyes. "I was merely expressing my dislike of America's consumerism over the summer." She heaves her bag over her shoulder. (Her Coach bag, I might add—so much for consumer elitism as an issue.)

"So what are you now? It's sort of an iCarly look."

"It's my look. The look that Claire Webber felt like wearing on the first day of senior year. People pleasing is a disease. Especially when it involves leaving a zit uncovered." Claire stomps off in her self-important way, still huffing over my insolence, and I follow willingly. "You should have hoofed it to 7-Eleven and got yourself some coverage. There's no excuse for this. You can blame your mother all you like, but there's no excuse for that kind of wimpiness. Your parents need to grow up. You need to train them!"

I won't mention the frilly pink prom journal just yet, but maybe she'll soften and understand my plight. Stranger things have happened.

"I just find it ironic that both you and my mother claim I shouldn't care what other people think, and yet both of you want to tell me exactly what I should think."

"Except I have your best interests at heart. I know you want more than to go to their Bible college of choice and find yourself a pastor for a husband."

"I'd appreciate it just the same if you'd let me make up my own mind."

"No you wouldn't." A cheerleader in uniform sneers at

Claire as she passes and hits Claire's shoulder with her own, knocking down her purse. Claire bends to pick it up. "Excuse you!" Claire yells. "Hey, you have toilet paper on your shoe." The cheerleader stops, examines her shoe, and offers one more snooty look before swaying away. Claire just laughs. "Let's go. I have Cooking first, what about you?"

"AP Calculus," I say.

"You know, it was one thing when you couldn't hang out with us at Starbucks, but you're months away from being an adult, Daisy. This is your last chance to fight for who you are, or you're going to end up like your mother."

I shudder at the thought. No offense, of course, but shoot me now!

Claire goes on. "I am not hanging out with you on the couch, screaming at the TV during game shows, for the rest of our lives. Soon enough you'll start knitting and taking in stray cats, and before you know it, we're desperate old women and these high school days will be the highlight of our lives. And look around you, Daisy. Our high school years sucked! I'm not going to do it."

"My mother is a good person. Besides, I can't sew. Or knit. And I don't like cats." I say this to remind myself, but I'm not forgetting that I have an enormous zit on display, or the same shirt I had on last year. We start walking the hallway, toward the math wing.

Claire is mumbling to herself. "If you were the type who didn't care that you have a giant zit on your forehead, fine. But you're not that person." Claire's exasperated with me, and her steps quicken. "I know you. You woke up and wanted to call in sick first thing."

"What are you so mad about this morning?"

"You promised this year would be different. All that bluster was another line."

"Bluster?"

"Quit changing the subject. I realize I have more freedom than most kids our age, but you have none, and the gulf is getting wider."

"But that has nothing to do with the spider ring?"

"Stop turning this back to me. Without me, your zit would be in class before you."

"It is different," I tell her. "I'm making myself goals. Not in an anal way, but in a directed, grown-up way. You know, to have more fun, just like we talked about."

Claire stops abruptly and gasps. "Where's your Abercrombie shirt?"

"Was that the bell?"

"Your mother slept around and survived it. She came to faith. Do they think you've learned nothing for yourself in twelve years of Christian school and weekly church?"

"She didn't sleep around!" As other kids stare at me, I lower my voice. "She only said she wasn't proud of her past."

"You're going to defend her. Don't you see? Nothing's changed, and you're going to be the same ghost of these hallways that you've always been. Why do they act like some sin is going to make you unworthy? Haven't they heard of rebellion? Or the fact that no one wants to sleep with you anyway?"

"Thanks." Sure, I knew my parents annoyed her, but I had no idea my lifestyle cramped hers. I consider confessing my prom journal to show proof that my inner rebellion has begun, but then I think that's just another form of people pleasing, so I take the lashing.

Claire groans. "I'll see you at lunch." She cinches the sash at her waist. "I can't be late for Cooking. I didn't eat breakfast and I'm starving." She stalks off toward class.

"You don't cook on the first day," I yell after her.

"See?" She turns toward me. "Total killjoy. Always quick with the facts, always making the lightest of circumstances completely serious. You would suck the fun out of Disneyland."

"I have a soy bar." I pull out one of my mother's health bars.

Claire walks back toward me. "What teenager carries soy bars in her bag?"

"The kind who meets the needs of her hungry best friend."

She snatches the bar. The first bell rings, and my feet start, but my body stays planted in the same place. "Daisy." Claire waves her hand in front of my face. "Look, I'm sorry. I shouldn't have been so mean, but I—"

"Chase Doogle is in the building," I say without moving my mouth.

Claire looks over her shoulder slyly. If there's anything we've perfected, it's the quiet-stalking gene. Sometimes our invisibility comes in handy.

Time stands still as he walks toward us. Claire sings like a ventriloquist through her clenched teeth, "He's hot but you're cold, you're yes but he's no."

Even Claire can't distract me. He looks the same, only broader, more manly. Like Almanzo from my *Little House* books, or how I imagine him anyway. Not like they show him on the Hallmark channel, but dark and beautiful with a farmhand's body. The rush of students stops as my ears fill with the beating of my own heart. Claire and I continue our conversation without moving our lips.

"Abercrombie or no, he will be mine."

"Downright scandalous!" Claire says. "Aren't you glad I keep makeup handy?"

"I owe you my life."

I open my mouth like I'm going to say something as he passes, but my backpack turns over as though by its own volition, and the contents tumble, splattering across the hallway. Some jock kicks my binder, and others play kick the can at the expense of my school supplies. The binder lands at Chase's feet. I don't look up. I simply stare at his Nike swoosh while I shove as much as I can into my backpack. Then I take my free hand to ensure my bangs are covering my forehead.

Chase lowers himself to the ground. He picks up as many items as possible and passes them to me. His hand brushes mine, and my body fills with endorphins.

He smiles. "Hi, Daisy."

"Hi, Chase." I venture a look at him, and his smile makes everything all right. He has the most amazing eyes. They make my entire body buzz with electrical forces no physics teacher could explain.

Then, to my horror, I spot it. My prom journal. I had shoved it in my backpack in case my mother got nosy. There it is, in all its pink glory, mercifully turned upside down on the ground. I practically dive to get it myself and shove it into my pack. I hit my head on the wall of lockers.

"You all right?" Chase asks. He helps me up.

"You've grown up over the summer." He stands well above the ice blue lockers with room to spare.

"Have I?"

"Your voice is lower."

"You all right, Daisy?" he asks again. "Don't forget, what goes around comes around."

"Huh?"

"Your backpack being thrown. You'd think some of these guys might have grown up by now."

"Oh." I look behind me. "Did it get thrown? I thought I'd just dropped it. I was focused on you. I mean, getting to class. I hadn't noticed." I rub the top of my head where I hit the lockers. Another bump is forming. The only way I seem to be growing. "I guess watching the contents dump out of one's backpack will always be funny to some people."

"Well, this is it, Daisy. Our last year together. I know you're going to do great things."

Somehow my last year with Chase doesn't bring me the comfort it brings him. "Yeah." I meet his delicious hazel eyes, which dance when he smiles. I'm lost in his gaze. If this is all I get, I'll take it. "I told my mother I was in love with you in kindergarten."

"I was in love with Miss Nelson," he says. "But you were a close second."

"My dad says close only counts in horseshoes."

"Miss Nelson broke my heart."

"Hey, Chase," Claire says. She didn't abandon me after all. "How was your summer? What'd you do, eat all summer? You grew. I never saw you at the club."

He pats his perfectly flat stomach—I know, I know, I shouldn't notice that kind of thing, but I'm human . . . and so very, very weak. "I went to boot camp with my father to train for the Air Force Academy."

"The Air Force Academy?" I ask.

54

"In Colorado. That's my plan."

"You've made plans," I stammer.

"Sure. Haven't you? I thought you were trying for some elite Ivy school all these years with your hard work."

I look at my feet. "Even if I wanted to go there, I couldn't pay for the first semester."

"That's what scholarships are all about. Didn't Miss Brody tell you to start applying for scholarships last year?"

"You remembered that?"

"I remembered because I was jealous!"

Claire clears her throat. "Yeah, so what happened at the Air Force Academy?"

"Not the academy, I went to survivalist camp in Colorado with my dad. I think he wanted to see how tough I was before he invested in the idea."

"Well, judging by the size of your pecs"—Claire pats Chase on the chest—"I'd say he'll get his money's worth."

"We spent a month learning to live in the wild. You should have seen me when I got back. I was emaciated. When I got home, I ate everything in sight. Of course then I vomited it all—" He stops mid-sentence. "Sorry. Too much information. Been around guys all summer. You can't imagine what it's like to forage for food in the mountains. Great stuff, but it sure makes you appreciate a stocked fridge."

Somehow, prom hardly matters when I think of Chase out of my life. The sting of tears pricks at the back of my nose.

"Daisy, you all right?" He feels the top of my head. "Maybe you should go to the office and get some ice for that."

"I'm fine."

He smiles down at me—kind of like I'm the "special" kid.

"So what did you two do all summer?"

"Oh you know, we hung out at the club, and Daisy here worked and read all of Shakespeare's plays. She probably did a little light reading and took on Tolstoy, right, Daisy?"

I swat Claire and lower my brows to tell her to shut up.

"What?" she says. "You did!" She turns to Chase. "Her mother is worried that her math mind can only go so far, so she's trying to turn her into the bard."

"Really?" Chase asks.

I give Claire the evil eye. "My mom wasn't thrilled with my English SAT score. She wanted me to be more well-rounded before I'm off to college." I spoke coherently! I'm so totally proud of myself, and it didn't sound forced either. I gather up a little confidence.

He nods. "That's cool. I had to ace the math portion too. Math is so important if I'm going to fly someday."

"Daisy's a walking calculator. You know how Spanish people think in Spanish and translate? Daisy thinks in numbers and turns them into words. She's great to shop with—she can tell you what 30 percent off of anything is."

"I've always loved your memory for numbers, Daisy. What's my phone number?"

"555-4988."

He shakes his head. "Totally amazing."

Not really.

"So you're going to learn to fly?"

"In a plane, Daisy. He hasn't sprouted wings over the summer," Claire says. "I have to get to Cooking class. Meet you out front at lunch, Daisy. Chase, good luck with that flying thing. I hear it's been great for Superman." Claire stomps off once she's lobbed the last word.

"I do hope I'm not going to be reciting emo poetry by the end of the day." I pray that more than the spider nose ring has vanished from Claire's summer of doom and conscience.

"What?" Chase asks. "Who's emo? Is anyone emo anymore?"

"No, no one's emo. I'm talking to myself—out loud."

"What do you have first?" Chase asks. Apparently, I don't answer soon enough because Chase asks again. "Daisy? Which class do you have first?"

"This is going to end."

"What?"

"We're going our separate ways."

"I can't keep up with you in the education department. I need to have a plan and get out of school."

"Sure, that's the point of school, right?"

He leans in and whispers in my ear. I feel the tickle to my toes. "I'm not a different person. It's still me, Daisy. I know you'll never forget my number, so you have no excuse not to call me in the future." He kisses me on the cheek, just like he did in kindergarten.

I look down at my cheap shoes and see a pair of heels in my line of sight. They're black, strappy heels, and the bearer has perfectly painted toes with a glitter flower on the big toe. The shoes stop beside me, and I let my line of sight follow the long legs up to long, blonde tresses and a smooth, china-doll face, absent of flaws.

"Hi, Chase!" The singsong voice of Amber Richardson hits my ears like nails on a chalkboard. She looks down at me from her lanky, mile-long body with her big head perched on top. "Claire."

"Daisy," I correct her. "Claire's my best friend."

"Are you talking to me? Because I think you've confused me with someone who cares." She fake laughs before checking Chase's reaction. "No, I'm totally kidding, don't look at me like that!" She shoves her wrist to my face. "Look what Chase bought me over the summer."

"Well, I didn't actually buy it," Chase says. "I negotiated it for her in Guatemala. We were there on the church mission trip," he explains.

Amber smirks at me. "How come you weren't there, Daisy? Don't you care that people don't have a church building to meet in? I mean, it's totally tragic!"

"I had to work all summer. I need a car for college." That sounds so much better than "my parents wouldn't let me do God's work alongside boys," and besides, it's true.

Amber is that girl who has it all: rich parents, cool clothes, perfect hair, student body something-or-other. Is it wrong to want to see her fall flat on her face? I'm thinking it is, since Jesus wouldn't want that, but whatever, it's still true. I'd still love to see that bleach-blonde hair splayed out on the concrete and her face looking up as though to say, "What happened?" Sort of like when your Mii is crushed after a Wii game. I want that look. So wrong, I know. I feel guilty, like I said, but I can still see her tresses in a splattered sunburst along the floor. I'm just not proud of it.

I look up into Chase's gorgeous eyes, and he's watching princess cheerleader blather on about something. Blah, blah, blah. Amber goes to our church, and she's in the popular group there too. I know there aren't supposed to be popular groups or cliques at church, but welcome to the real world. I'm a nobody at school, and surprise—I'm a nobody at church too. God may not care that my jeans aren't designer, but his teenage people sure seem to.

"OMG!" princess cheerleader shouts, breaking me from thought. She actually says O-M-G like she's Hannah Montana or something. "I totally have History first too!" She shakes her paper like it's a winning lottery ticket. Knowing Amber, she probably hacked into the school computer and listed all the guys she wanted to "own" that year, and stalked their classes. Chase has been "mine" all these years—well, with the exception of sharing him with Miss Nelson. Completely off the radar of cool girls like Amber, and now he goes and grows like a stalk of corn over the summer, and suddenly he's visible to girls.

Life is so not fair. I mentally list the other four guys on my prom list. It doesn't have to be Chase. It doesn't! But he's not going with Amber either. As God is my witness, I will protect him from those manicured claws.

My chest deflates over the fact that Chase and Amber have homeroom together, not that it was all that inflated in the first place, but it looked more inflated in that Abercrombie shirt, which is now with the angels. Or back at Goodwill, depending on if my mother felt strongly enough to "spare" another family the trouble.

The silence grows, and the three of us shift, wondering who is going to break the unbearable "third wheel" scene. Naturally, it's Amber.

"So Claire, you, like, totally grew too. I think you're taller than last year, if that's possible, but I don't think you gained a pound. Oh my gosh, you could almost be a model for, like, one of those concentration camp pictures." She flips her hair. "I'm so jealous!" She presses her bulbous, red, glossy lips together. "Your hair got bigger, though! No blonde highlights or tan?" She manipulates her head to stare at the back of mine.

"Gosh, that makes me so sad. Where'd you have to work? The freezer at Safeway?" She laughs again and touches my wrist. "I'm totally kidding, but it's like you got no sun. You're like my Q-tip after I've taken my mascara off with it. Black, wild head, but still as albino as before summer."

I will myself to keep silent on the fact that Q-tips were invented in 1923. It will only give Amber more ammunition. Chase doesn't seem to notice any of Amber's barbs. What is with guys? They want to believe a beautiful girl's heart is just as pretty as the outside. Don't they have mothers?

"Daisy's lucky. She can eat anything she wants and keep that body," Chase says with a smile. "Her complexion has always been like that."

My hand immediately flies to my forehead, and I know he's given Amber more to run with. I'm not good at the kind of conversation that involves a deeper level, meant to sabotage your every word. Where is Claire when I need her?

And then, one of my horrible facts comes spilling out of my mouth. It's like I can't help myself, I need the attention—but bad attention is not a good thing. "Did you know Kraft makes enough Cool Whip every year to fill up the Grand Canyon?"

"Fascinating and yet so very pointless. Chase, we totally have to get to class. Well, see ya, Claire."

"Daisy," I say halfheartedly.

"Right. I keep forgetting. You girls are so alike!" Amber clutches Chase's arm again, but he wrangles out of her grip. "I'll catch up with you in class, Amber. I had something I wanted to ask Daisy."

"Oh, right, sure," she says, but she doesn't move.

Hello, clueless, I do believe he has something to ask ME.

I'm hopeful that Chase is already planning for prom. I mean, maybe he's worried that I'll get swooped up, and he wants to ensure that our last moments together are certain.

"Chase," she says in baby talk, while walking her fingers up Chase's arm. "I wanted to talk to you about the Air Force Academy. Remember we talked about Daddy giving you his recommendation." She turns to me. "My dad is a senator, you know."

"Mine dresses like a duck."

"What?" Amber's face screws up. "Okay, whatever. Chase, my dad totally wants to meet you. After he found out what you did for me in Guatemala, he was totally into the rec-ommendation." Amber looks at me again. "You know, you need a letter of recommendation from either a senator or a representative."

"I didn't know that. It's forever implanted up here now, though," I say, tapping my temple. I'm filing it under *skeevy*.

Chase gives me an apologetic smile. "You don't mind, do you, Daisy? It wasn't important, and this is the final thing I need."

"No, sure. You can't be a flyboy without that."

"You rock." Amber starts walking away, which forces Chase to run after her in some lame attempt to make it appear he's making an awkward play for her stone-cold heart. "Amber, wait up!"

I'm still watching when the bell rings. "Shoot! Now I'm dissed and late."

He left. With her! Amber, one. Daisy, zero.

❧ 5 ❧

Prom Journal
September 9
177 Days until Prom
Fact: Susan Boyle, with the voice of an angel, still plucked herself bare and bought lipstick before her next appearance.

    If at first you don't succeed, you probably need a makeover. My mom says I'm getting vain. The makeup argument continued when my third eye refused to disappear. Contraband Amazing Base saved me. I believe in its power.

    My mom recited the "beauty is fleeting, charm is deceiving" proverb while I tried to fix my bangs to cover the boil until I got to the school bathroom. I would totally believe that proverb if the male race believed it, but it seems someone forgot to tell them. The guy's version would be, "Beauty is fleeting, so you want to grab it up now, before the next guy gets it. The prettier she is, the more points for you. Go!"

I am becoming neurotic. This much is true. Maybe I always was and just put my neuroses into schoolwork, and now that I've slacked off a little, all that neurotic energy has to go somewhere. School was so much easier because I could actually succeed at that, but being known, getting a guy to notice me as more than his math tutor . . . that's a whole 'nother story. Here's the rundown.

1. ~~Brian Logan.~~ He's dating Heather Wells, and judging by where I saw his hand today, he's no longer an option.

2. Steve Crisco. He's in my Calculus class, which he wouldn't be in if it weren't for me. He sat right next to me to assure himself a good grade. So he's moved down the list. Is it rude if I ask my date to take an IQ test? Tired of surfing stories already.

3. Greg Connolly. Still doesn't know I exist as a female. Told him that there were more than 80 recorded spellings of Shakespeare's name in English and he stared at me funny. Like I might snap at any moment. Hello? Were we not in English Lit? Totally relevant?

4. Kelvin Matthews. I think the gel hands are going to get to me. Why am I so shallow?

5. Chase Doogle. I've saved the worst news for last. He did call me. Because he was working at Claire's club

at the end of the season. He found my sweatshirt in the lost and found, and rather than give it to Goodwill, he brought it home. I haven't quite given up on the fact that he was trying to stake his claim for prom. I mean, he could have told me about the sweatshirt in front of Amber.

My mother's homemade sweatshirt reads, "Made with love by Molly Crispin," and then my name is sprawled beneath in red Sharpie. It had my name ironed in the collar, like I was four. So humiliating. I would have totally lied and said it wasn't mine, but tell me, what choice did I have? He's going to bring it to school for me.

While I'm dreaming of our perfect prom photos, which I would show to our grandchildren, Chase is thinking, "Even with her lame label, Daisy can't keep track of her clothes. And it's not like she has a lot of them—isn't that the same sweatshirt she wore for three years?"

Chase is working on making "Top Gun" his future, and I'm still trying to get "plays well with others" under control. Daisy Doogle is a distant dream. I don't know, maybe that's a good thing, but right now, as Amber makes her latest spidery move, I must say, it sucks to be me.

Dates turned down: 0
Dates offered to turn down: 0
Most embarrassing random fact I blurted out during Physics:

Count von Count of *Sesame Street* is based on the legend that throwing seeds at vampires wards them off. Vampires were compelled to count the seeds.

Like I said, sucks to be me.

When I was in elementary school, there was this red line painted across the blacktop. If you were in the third grade or below, you couldn't cross that red line and descend into the big-people world of the fourth through sixth graders. The magical mystery of what lay beyond that line mesmerized me, like if I could only step into that world, as if pixie dust were suddenly under my feet, I would ascend into a different hemisphere.

Naturally, when I got to fourth grade, I saw that things looked exactly the same on the other side of the line, but it was the intrigue of the unknown that made it so off-limits and terrifyingly fascinating.

St. James Academy has that line too. I'll call it the PE (popular equator), only it's invisible and causes strange happenings of polar proportions. It's like *Lost* for the high school set. It takes a certain kind of person to venture into the realm of popular kids. Haven't figured out what kind of person that is, I only know my group isn't that.

Those of us on the other side of the equator are not privy to the conversations about upcoming events and certainly are not on the guest list for the parties. Like being on the wrong side of the blacktop, we are left to wonder about the magical happenings yonder.

❧ ■ ❧

"Four days of school down," Claire says. "How many to go, Daisy?"

"Not counting weekends or vacation days, 176."

"The home stretch." Claire laughs and tosses her lunch onto the grass. Our ragtag group of friends is back together, having lunch on the back lawn, sitting crisscross-applesauce in a circle, like we always have.

A mere four days into the school year, Claire is completely over her summer goth stage and is now very J.Crew-looking. The hallway light didn't do her makeover justice. Her hair is back to brown with salon caramel highlights in a wedged bob, and her nails are manicured and painted an electric blue. She pulls her lunch out of the sack (a can of strawberry Slim-Fast) and toasts us. "To us! Seniors at last."

"To us," we echo.

"To my friends," I say, lifting my Snapple. "People who understand my need to share random facts."

"I wouldn't say we understand it, I'd say we deal with it," Angie says. "It's weird to us too."

There are four of us altogether. Claire and I met the other two as freshmen in Chorale. "We've come a long way since Chorale," Claire says. With our choir robes and red, rubber headbands, we had no idea that only freshmen nerds joined the a cappella choir.

"Oh my gosh, had we known," Angie says with a laugh. "Remember how we walked out all proud of our choir robes, only to be met by the dance team in the *Dancing with the Stars* hot chick outfits?" Angie laughs.

"It seared our friendship," I say.

"And our reputations," Claire adds.

"Always the pessimist," I tell her.

"Realist."

"Pessimists always call themselves realists," Angie says.

Angie Chen is first-generation American, which explains why she didn't know *choir* was a pseudonym for *nerd*. (Still wondering what my excuse was. Too many seasons of *American Idol*, perhaps?) Angie's parents are from Shanghai, so she goes to Chinese school on Saturdays, plays the piano like Mozart, and has less of a social life than me. Chorale hardly cramped her style, but the great thing about Angie is she never cared. She's too practical to worry about prom or high school crushes. Oh, that I could be like her.

"Claire calls herself whatever she likes. You're never going to enlighten her about a thing," Sarika says, and because she rarely says much, her comment stops Claire cold.

Sarika Singh was born in southern India but moved here in high school. Her parents (dad Indian, Mom white) run a church and minister to those from the Hindu faith. Her father also owns some high-tech business and imports Indian engineers like souvenirs. Her family is vegetarian, which I could totally do if my mom cooked like hers, but alas, turmeric is not a spice used in our home. Salt is considered living on the wild side and is not added without my father's cholesterol number being announced aloud.

"Do you think we've come a long way?" Sarika asks. "I was just here thinking we are exactly like we were four years ago. I want a boyfriend this year. You know how when a guy goes off to war, he wants someone waiting? I feel that way about college. You can't be marriage material unless you're involved."

"What?" I shout. "You want a boyfriend? Oh my gosh, that's so completely normal, Sarika. I thought I was the only one of us."

"Seriously, when you're attached, it makes you unattainable. My dad says guys love that."

"Your dad wants you to have a boyfriend?" I ask her. "That does not sound like your dad."

"No, he wasn't talking about me! But you girls. You should get a boyfriend before you go to college. That way, you can trade up."

"He's not a used car," I say.

"You mean I can't kick the tires?" Claire jokes. "You would have a boyfriend, Daisy, if you'd stop dressing like the girl all men over eighty fantasize about, who brings them their orange juice."

"That's not the reason," Angie says. "It's the fact that she cannot keep her mouth shut about how many hearts an octopus has and other encyclopedic facts."

I stand up. "Come on, it's time for lunch assembly. We get to go into the popular world for assembly in the gym."

"We can be fashionably late," Claire says. "Those assemblies are lame anyway. We're seniors. We know the rules by now."

We all stare at one another after this assessment. "But we always go to the assemblies," I say.

"So today, we'll do something different," Claire says.

Angie, the optimist of us, speaks up. "We did do something different. We're not completely the same. Claire got a better haircut. Sarika's face cleared up, and Daisy, you grew five inches at least."

"That's not what I meant," Claire says.

"I'm not the same person I was in Chorale," I say.

"No, now we see your clothes," Claire quips. "Lucky us."

"That was cold," Angie says.

I look down at my "uniform" and suddenly feel empowered. "No, she's right, Angie. I look exactly the same." I shake my head. "You don't get it. You're all going out into the great, wide world and I'm going to Bible college."

"There's nothing wrong with Bible college," Sarika states, which is easy to say since she's going to Stanford.

"I've been in Bible school kindergarten through senior year. Is it wrong to want something different? Where are you applying, Claire?"

She shrugs. "The UC system."

"You need that extracurricular for San Diego or Berkeley," Angie tells her. "Good thing you've got tennis." Then she looks at me. "They count work experience, Daisy. For kids who had to work instead of play."

All three of them look at me. "Seriously, I would consider Bible college if my parents' goal wasn't to get me married off to a preacher."

"You'll get into any school you want," Claire says. "No preacher would marry you. Don't they know about your Tourette's with facts? You'd empty the pews in no time."

"Let's go. We're going to be late for assembly." I sling my backpack over my shoulder and start walking. Angie and Sarika pack up, and Claire finally gives up and throws her empty Slim-Fast can in the bag.

"Don't you want to go out with a bang? Be remembered for more than—I don't know—sitting here on the grass by ourselves?" Claire asks. "There's a big world out there!" She stretches her arms out.

"A big, bitter world that's told us we don't matter," I say. Why mention I have the very same goal? Then it wouldn't be Claire's idea and I wouldn't have her full cooperation.

They all shake their heads in unison. "I can't wait to get

out of here," Sarika says. "I'm sick of high school. I am tired of people who care about what clothes you wear more than your accomplishments in life."

"I agree. I can hardly wait to get out," Angie says.

"That's because you all have a place to go." Unsaid: *Hello? What about me?*

"You've earned the money to put yourself through school. You've hoarded everything you've earned. And it's not like you won't work during college. You know how to juggle both already." Claire sniffs.

I don't mention that I've applied to Pepperdine's prestigious business school and my "hoarding" barely covers books, much less tuition.

"You could have afforded to dress well if you wanted to," Sarika says.

"It doesn't seem very responsible to choose clothes over college."

"Don't bother with her, girls, she's convinced she has to save every penny she earns. She has an answer for every one of your suggestions. If she breaks into the piggy bank now, everything is doomed."

Claire just described my parents, and I scramble to remember why I save everything. "Um, junior college, my parents . . . living at home. Should I elaborate?"

"Oh, right," Angie says.

Just the way she says it is depressing. Like everyone knows my parents are the strictest. Sarika's parents want to choose whom she marries, and Angie's want her to become a doctor before she's married, yet they're all mourning *my* life. That's just sad.

"So are we going to try to fit in once before we leave?"

"I don't care if I'm popular," Claire states. "You can't be popular and cheap, Daisy. You can't pay for college and dress like Amber Richardson, so why compete on a level like that? Don't you watch *The Hills*? That crowd is vicious. You're the smart girl, Daisy. Just accept it."

"Hey, Daisy!"

I look behind me and shield my eyes against the sun, and Greg Connolly (#3 on my list) is walking toward us. "Hi, Greg," I say, while desperately gulping the remaining PB and J in my mouth. Dang. I'm a spaz. I remind myself to offer no facts. Prom princesses do not know that Greg's height could merely be a malfunction of the pituitary gland.

"Can I talk to you for a minute?" Greg asks, looking at the rest of my friends. "Alone?"

"Sure." I could swear Claire scowls at me, but I follow Greg. "What's up?"

Greg looks like Orlando Bloom and dresses like a J.Crew ad. No, he dresses like a J.Crew *catalog*! I whip my head around toward Claire, with her sweater thrown leisurely over her shoulders in a knot and her hair pushed back by a plaid headband, and suddenly the ground feels a bit shaky. Why do I remember random facts but don't see what's right in front of me?

He looks around me, back toward the group, and my fears are confirmed. "Claire's not been coming to youth group at church. Was she gone this summer? She didn't even come for food-pantry stocking. She always comes to that."

Because I drag her!

"No, her mother and father have been away. They don't like her to leave the house at night when they're gone. The maid gets afraid. But I haven't been coming either." Implication: did you notice my absence, Greg?

"Oh," he stammers, and kicks his toe into the grass.

"Is there something you wanted to ask me about Claire, Greg?"

He shrugs. "I don't know. I thought we'd . . . I don't know . . . connected over the summer. Earlier, at the club. Now she doesn't talk to me."

"She'll be at youth group soon."

I walk back to my friends, and Claire has one eyebrow raised. I can't help but feel slightly betrayed. I would have never written Greg's name in my prom journal had I known they were a possibility. "You don't tell your friends when you're flirting with intent?" I ask her.

"What?" Claire asks.

"He asked about you, Claire. I didn't ask you anything about the goth phase, just let it slide, but if this J.Crew phase has anything to do with Greg, I'd wish you'd said something." I settle back into our dysfunctional circle as we walk.

"Me? Why on earth would Greg ask about me?" She places her hand on the knot of her sweater.

"I can't fathom," I say with a smirk.

The gym is packed when we get inside, only because attendance is mandatory. The only seats that remain are in the front, next to all the freshmen.

"I told you we'd be late," I say.

"I told us not to come," Claire says. "No one takes roll."

We pile into the available seats in the second row, and the overhead lights dim. The school band plays some praise song that is unrecognizable with the blare of the horns and off-key, out-of-practice musicians.

Principal Walker, looking tidy and uptight in his gray suit, knocks on the microphone, and the band quits as they see fit. The speakers overload, and the students groan.

"Good afternoon, students of St. James Academy. It's been a fine year so far, but we'd like to keep it that way throughout the year. One of the things we pride ourselves on here at St. James is the quality of peer communication and the lack of bullying that goes on in our hallways."

"Yeah, if you're the principal," I say.

"Today we are very fortunate to have a group of guests who have come to teach us what can happen when there is no respect in the hallways. Bullying is not tolerated in our school, nor should it be in any Christian environment, but this is one more way we'd like to drive the message home. Please help me welcome Mr. and Mrs. Crispin and their troupe as they act out 'Pretty in Peer Pressure.'"

My face goes white, and I do believe my PB and J is backing up on me. My friends look at me, and I shrug and shake my head. *Please, please, let it be another Mr. and Mrs. Crispin.* Surely I have some long-lost relatives in the area.

The music starts with "Girls Just Want to Have Fun," and my mother bops out dressed as Cyndi Lauper, twisting her skirt with zeal as she skips across the stage. It might even be her hideous, hot pink dress from prom. Only now it's just a skirt, because let's face it, my mom is no girl, and her dance could easily be confused for the dry heaves.

I shut my eyes, hoping it will be over soon, but I hear the word *puberty*, followed by *purity*, and then the roar of laughter in the audience. My face is hot, and I sink as low as I can into my chair without sliding onto the wood floor.

The music of the first act wilts, and my father appears on

stage, dressed as Elvis. His sideburns are a rich, glossy black, and I can only pray the kids think it's part of his costume.

"We need a volunteer!" my dad bellows.

To my horror, I hear my mom shout, in her Cyndi Lauper voice, "Chase Doogle, why don't you come on up?"

I turn to see my crush running toward the stage. It's all very surreal, as though I'm in a bad nightmare and I'm suddenly going to wake up to find it was all my imagination—my terribly vivid, perfect, spot-on, searing imagination. I shut my eyes tight, hoping when I open them, this will all go away.

"Chase," my mother says to the audience, "has known my daughter since kindergarten. Daisy, stand up and say hello."

I keep my eyes shut. Spontaneous human combustion. Dickens said it happened in *Bleak House*. It could happen. Or the Rapture, that could happen, and I'd float away happily, never looking down.

"Yoo-hoo! Daisy, wake up!" my mother calls.

I am slunk down as far as I can be without being on the floor. I open my eyes and shoot her the stare of my life. *Please, Mother. I'll never ask for anything again.*

"Our daughter Daisy . . ." My father continues in his Elvis voice with his tilted lip and popped collar. He's the old Elvis. The fat one who OD'd, who is hardly the model for a talk on self-restraint. Or bullying, or whatever this hot mess is about. "She says no one at this school knows her, but that isn't true. We all feel like we don't fit in, and it's hard to trust those around us. That's why we wrote this play about the trials of peer pressure, so you could know you're not alone."

My mom meets my gaze again. "You're not alone."

I may not be alone, but how I wish to high heaven I was at this juncture.

My dad rips off his Elvis jacket, slaps on a baseball cap, and flips it backward. My mother rips off her red wig. She's wearing some form of Lego hair that appears snapped onto the top of her head. She flicks her suspenders on her shoulders, and they're joined by two young break-dancers in saggy jeans. Rap music pulsates throughout the gym. Chase backs away slowly.

"Yo! Yo!" my dad chants directly at Chase. "I may not be cool or dress like you, but I got deep feelings roiling round in me too." He hammers his hands toward the ground and back at his chest. "Yo! Yo! Don't want to be a label sleaze. Hear me out, I dress as I please. Don't judge me by my size, shape, or color. I am the way God made me."

"I'm so tall!"

"I'm too short!"

"My face is a wreck!"

"I might as well be invisible!"

"That's how we roll. That's just how we roll!" the chorus goes.

It continues, painfully, for a full ten minutes. I can't watch! All I can remember is something about getting jiggy with it and how we roll.

When it's over, I'm numb.

Claire grins. "Well, you're not invisible now. Be careful what you wish for."

"Are they kidding me? I can't go to a dance, but my parents can sing in front of the entire school and get jiggy with it?"

Sarika shrugs. "That's just how we roll." She starts to laugh.

I rush out the door, but I'm surrounded by students and

get stopped in the crowd. There are so many talking at me, I get only tidbits.

"So cool!"

"That rocked!"

"I wish I had parents like that!"

"You're so lucky!"

I scramble away with Claire next to me. "Did you hear that? I'm lucky to have deranged parents? Are they kidding?"

Claire's expression turns somber. "In some ways, you are. It wasn't that bad, Daisy. It was kind of cute."

"Shut up."

"Seriously, it was. Besides, no one knows who you are. What are the chances they know you're their daughter?"

"Daisy!"

"Shh!" I snap at the sound of my name. "People will know who I am!" I turn to see a guy following us out of the gym. "Do I know you?"

"Your parents just pointed you out," he says.

My life is over.

"I don't think so." Suddenly I'm Peter denying Jesus, and the guilt overwhelms me. "Yeah, I'm Daisy."

As the stranger approaches, I see he's about the same height as me, maybe a tad shorter. He's tanned like a Spanish warrior with dark chocolate eyes, cropped hair, and seriously cute dimples. He has a regal, Spanish-royalty look to him, and I could easily picture him in a brightly colored uniform with gold buttons.

"Did you know dimples are actually a birth defect? The result of a shortened muscle." I did not just say that.

His hand covers his left cheek, and I feel Claire slap my back.

"Hi, I'm Claire." She thrusts out her hand, but I push it away.

"Isn't Greg looking for you?" I ask her.

"Excuse my friend, she spouts useless trivia when she gets nervous. Which I take to mean she finds you cute. If she starts talking numbers, I'd run. See ya." Claire bops off like the traitor she is. Chase is standing by the gym doorway staring at us. He shakes his head and disappears back into the gym, fighting the exiting students like a salmon swimming upstream.

I look back at the dimples in front of me.

"You're blushing." He laughs, and his dimples appear in full.

I feel my cheeks. "Too much sun, I guess."

"I wanted to introduce myself. I'm Max." He rakes his hand through that gorgeous black hair. "I wanted to say that no one knows me either. So now we know each other. I thought maybe that would do us both good."

"Well, Max, maybe I can show you the ropes of being an unknown. I assume you're at least new?"

"Yeah." He looks back toward the gym. Chase is standing beside Amber—who is pointing at me and laughing. "Maybe your days of anonymity are over. I wanted to say 'hey' before that happened."

"I don't think you have to worry about that." I keep talking to Max, but I can't take my eyes off Amber's flirtatious stance. "Good things don't happen to me."

"What?" Max asks.

I meet his deep brown eyes to force my attention away from Chase. "Do you ever feel like the Lord uses you for comic relief? I'm an understudy." I'm talking to myself more than

Max, but he lifts my chin with his thumb so my attention is fully on him.

"Only Satan would make you believe such a thing."

"Where'd you come from?"

"The public school down the street. They didn't offer AP History and I need it for my major. I'm going to pray for you, Daisy. You're not looking at the right things."

"They have that accent at the public school?"

"Oh, you meant where did I originally come from." He laughs. "Argentina. I'll catch up with you later. I just wanted to introduce myself before you disappeared into the crowd."

That. Is. What. I. Do. Best.

He starts walking across the quad. "I have to get to wood shop."

"Wait, Max! What's your last name?"

"Diaz!" he yells back. "And I find you cute too, Daisy Crispin! Save a few random facts for me, okay?"

❧ 6 ❧

Checks R Us is a check-printing company, and my employer has a horrible track record for quality. The employees screw things up in the factory. I get yelled at in the office. Interesting system, but it pays well. Banks, customers—pretty much anyone who needs to vent—has my number and an issue. It's good practice for school since no one seems to notice I'm an actual person there either. Until today, when I'm an actual person with parents who rap. Oh, the shame of it!

When I started this job, I seriously thought about not going to college rather than pursuing my mother's dream of me marrying a preacher. Then I did the math of listening to cranky bank tellers until I was sixty-five, and my head about exploded. So I applied like a madwoman for any and *every* college that would accept me.

My co-workers are still on the phone, taking their own rash of crap. The thing about people yelling at you? They don't want to be put on hold while they scream because they might lose momentum, and they're like a torrent of steam or a freight train that will bear down on you. Not pretty. There's usually some coarse language involved and lots of soothing words on my part. I might consider a career in wild animal training.

I adjust my headset and answer the phone. "Checks R Us, this is Daisy speaking. How may I help you today?"

"Daisy, this is Bev at Wells Fargo. Our customer received an order with someone else's address, and this is not the first time it's happened."

Nor will it be the last, Bev. Apparently you're not familiar with our company. "Bev, I'm terribly sorry about that. There must have been a mix-up in the plant. Let me get that reordered right away."

Everyone's off the phone at this point, staring at me while I finish. We're at our ancient metal desks, arranged in four-square order, and the phones have died down. Friday afternoon at the banks has started. Very few of the banks complain on Friday because they're too busy to call us.

"Hi, everybody."

"So . . . how's school?" Lindy, my supervisor, is head customer-service rep. She's from Peru, tiny, serious-natured, and supports her family (including her mom and sisters) with this crappy job. She's also the youngest besides me, but the most mature—which isn't saying much. She takes her job seriously but puts up with the rest of us. And our need to vent. Lindy is the type of girl who brushes past all the negativity on the line with her very genuine friendliness. "You made it through your first week."

"School is the same. Lots of homework, plenty of fashionistas, not much fun." I decide not to venture into the territory of my parents bustin' a rhyme.

"Who cares about that? Any cute guys this year?" Kat asks. "We keep hoping for you, honey."

"If there are guys, they're nowhere near me."

"Oh, honey, you come to Kat and I'll get you all set up. Such a pretty girl like you, so smart and all. You should have a boyfriend."

"She's not allowed to have a boyfriend," Lindy reminds her.

"I've never heard of such a thing. My son has had girl-friends her age," she says. "You gonna be a nun, honey?"

Her son also lives with her and has a baby mama, but that's hardly the point. There has to be some middle ground. At least, that's what I keep telling myself. The world is not black and white. Despite what my parents think. Despite what Claire thinks.

"It's a quiet day," Lindy says. "We had that mad rush there, but otherwise it's been very quiet all day. I think Gil had some numbers he wanted you to check too."

A moment later Kat slams down the phone. "I ain't show-ing no public school moron my paystub to take no handout. They can kiss my derriere."

Kat's a single mother and smells like an ashtray with a chaser of stale coffee. She wears a cheap perfume to cover the odor, but honestly, the sharp stench is worse. But if you're ever in a battle? You want Kat on your side. She is the sweet-est lady, but she could probably take on Evander Holyfield, so if I didn't work with her, I wouldn't know the kind heart that lurks behind her linebacker presence. In fact, if I met her on the street, I'd probably cross it to avoid a confronta-tion. Don't like what that says about me, but I'm glad she's on my side.

"You getting your homework done with this job, Daisy?" Kat asks. "You work so much. You should take it easy."

I nod. "Not really an option in my house. All my parents have to keep up with is me, so they tend to check on me regularly."

"You get your education, baby. You don't want to do this kind of job forever. Your parents know all about it. You find a job you love and every day is like a party." She pauses to hack a few minutes. "That's what they tell me anyway."

Gil comes out of his office. "What's all this talking? You girls file if the phones are quiet!" He reminds me of the young teacher trying to earn respect. He barks most everything but then waits to see if he's been heard. If we ask him a question, he gets flustered and acts as though he already made himself clear.

Gil Keegan is the owner's son. He cannot stand to watch anyone sit still—it's a personal affront to him. He's stuck in this job because his father has bigger fish to fry, and Gil's determined to feed his ego from the job, if nothing else. He's darling, though, only twenty-four, recently out of college, and he looks like Josh Lucas. When he talks, no matter what he says or how rude he sounds, I find myself drifting into the movie *Sweet Home Alabama* and seeing the prince hiding behind the redneck. Or, in this case, the prince behind the powerless owner's son. Hey, my dream life helps me get through the day, all right?

Anyway, Gil is cute, achingly so. And if he laid a hand on me, both our fathers would kill us, so there is this unrequited, Shakespearian thing going on between us. My mom would love it in a book. Not so much with me as the star.

Gil spends the majority of his time on Maple Story pretending to be married to some character from Japan. I can't tell you how many times I've had to run out to 7-Eleven to pick him up a game card so he can buy a pet, or a house, or something to succeed in his imaginary world. I sure hope it's better than this world for him, because this one seems tedious.

"Daisy, you have a minute?" Gil asks. He turns back to my co-workers. "Get to work if the phones aren't ringing."

Kat doesn't even bother to wait for him to leave the room before bursting into her trademark cackle.

I look around. "It's your minute," I tell him as I follow him into his office.

"Sit down," he says as he sits behind his desk. He pulls out a ledger with pencil markings dating back to another decade. "I tried to make a spreadsheet for this, and nothing is adding up. I need this information entered into a computer so I can analyze the numbers."

I nod.

"Naturally, this will be between us."

"It's okay, Gil. I assume you make money from the Porsche you drive. How much is none of my business."

His lagoon-colored eyes narrow. "How'd you get so good at numbers at your age?"

"I used to play office as a kid. I'd find my dad's bills in one place, invoices in another. I started organizing them at five, my mother says. They bought me a computer, and by ten, I was doing my father's invoicing. I learned early that it's always good to have money in the account to pay your bills."

"Necessity is the mother of invention."

"I like order," I say. "My parents not so much."

"Sounds like we were both born into the wrong families. It's no wonder my father found you."

I reach for the pale green ledgers.

"Not now," Gil says. "I need you to do it after hours."

"Gil, I have homework. A lot of it."

"I'll pay you."

"Don't say that." My perfectionist tendencies cannot stand to turn down money. The more I make, the more freedom I have. The more freedom I have, the less my parents can make all my decisions.

"Daisy, this company is in dire straits. That's why my dad handed it to me. Those people out there need this job, and I need to prove to my father I can do this if I'm ever going to get out of here."

"Overtime?" I ask, knowing this is asking for trouble. "It's a pain to take the bus after dark."

He shakes his head. "I can't believe your parents won't let you date, but they let you take the bus home at night. It makes no sense."

I shrug. "I can't believe you work here and drive a Porsche. We're all mysteries."

"Touché."

I sound so calm, but I need this job. The money is all I have to keep me going and get me out from under my parents' grasp. Lindy and Kat have qualifications and time. I don't. Whether at school or in my small workforce, I am at the bottom of the food chain.

"I can either work over the weekend or start Monday." I look down at the ledgers. "I'm finishing the last of my college applications."

"I want a nice, clean spreadsheet with columns, every row labeled. I need to know when the company started to tank and any market analysis—" He stops talking. "I'm not making a lick of sense to you, am I?"

His dismissal of me for being a mere student irritates me. "I'll do my own analysis as well. We'll compare notes."

"Monday is fine. Tell your dad to pick you up. You're not taking the bus that late. If he doesn't, I'll be taking you home, and somehow I doubt he'll like seeing you roll up with a man in a Porsche."

"You're offering to take me home in the Porsche?" I laugh.

"Oh no. One wrong move and you're driving my Porsche. I remember that old police song about the young schoolgirl. I'm not as dumb as all that. Just use it as a threat, all right? The thought of me driving Miss Daisy should make him crazy."

I wish, just for one second, I could speak as easily to the guys at school as I can to Gil. I'm here at work, I know the business, I know the numbers. I know the benefits of everything going into neat little rows and columns, but school isn't like that. There's an entire set of rules that no one ever tells you. Disorder lurks around every corner. Mean girls flipping your backpacks, dense jocks cheating off you in Calculus. The world seems like a much safer place after high school.

I pick up the books and put them back in Gil's metal filing cabinet, twist the lock, and hand him the key. "You need to hire an accountant. And maybe someone who speaks English out in the plant but actually reads it too. Today I had a complaint that someone wrote 'deceased' on the check."

"Again?" Gil shakes his head. He's got Zac Efron hair and sparkling bluish-green eyes. The kind of eyes that my mother should warn me about, instead of her having kittens over an Abercrombie shirt. All I'm saying.

Gil pauses, leans back in his chair, and narrows his eyes. "You're a bossy little thing, you know that?"

"But I'm good at ledgers and I'm cheaper than an accountant."

"Mouthy too. I'm going to tell your school advisor how mouthy you are when I give my review. 'Works hard,'" he writes on a pad of paper as he says it. "'Needs to shut up.'"

"Gil, you can't stop with the ledgers. You've got to get these orders all computerized—an online ordering system for the banks. The business is going to be gone if we're not up and running soon. When these paper orders come through, they're nearly always wrong, and these ledgers would be a lot easier to read if you—" His eyes are glazing over, and I'm losing him to some computerized game he's obsessing over. "At the very least, the reprints would cost the banks instead of us."

He gives his bad-boy smile and leans forward. "I'm planning to, Miss Daisy. I've been reviewing systems and webmasters; that's why I need this place cleaned up. That all right with you?" He stands and opens the door to his office for me to exit. "Did you notice how you said 'us'? You take ownership, Daisy, and that's what all bosses want to see in their employees. What if college isn't the right avenue for you? Did you ever think about that?"

"I can never tell if you take me seriously or if you're making fun of me."

"A little of both, maybe." He flips his hair and leans against the wall. "You and Lindy take on a lot for me. Just know that I appreciate it, and someday, when I'm first in check printing, I won't forget it."

I stare at him intently.

"What?" he asks with a laugh. "Why do you keep looking at me like that? Say something. Don't stare at me like I've got three heads."

"Why are you here?" I ask him. "Why do you work for your father?"

"A man's gotta start somewhere."

I stand outside Gil's office for a second, wondering why I'm so comfortable here in this place with complete strangers, and then it dawns on me. This is the one place in the world I can truly be myself. And how sad is that? Maybe college isn't for me. Maybe Gil's right. What if it's only a continuation of high school?

I peek my head in Gil's doorway again.

"Did you forget something?" he asks.

"Gil, did you go to your prom?"

"My high school prom?" he asks over his monitor.

"Uh-huh." I feel stupid now, but it's out there. "Did you ask someone to prom?"

"Sure. My girlfriend. Actually, I don't know that I asked. She just told me what color tie to get and where to get a limo. I did as I was told."

"Oh, you had a girlfriend." I sigh.

"Daisy?"

"Yeah?"

"You can always ask him if he doesn't ask you. Isn't prom in the spring?"

"Yeah, I'm thinking ahead. I can ask him. Yeah." I turn away, annoyed at the suggestion, but then face him again before I lose my nerve. "But——"

"You have to let him know you like him, Daisy. Guys don't like rejection any more than girls do. Have you flirted with him at all?"

"I don't know how to flirt."

He laughs. "Yes you do."

87

"Amber Richardson has let him know, and I don't think I can do that."

"If Amber's let him know and he hasn't made a move, he's not interested in Amber." Gil shrugs. "Let him know, Daisy. We just need encouragement."

I nod. Sure. It's just my heart at stake. No biggie, right?

Prom Journal

September 10

176 Days until Prom

330 Days Left in Captivity (until I Leave for College!)

Fact: 14 percent of young adult men live at home compared to 8 percent of women. Sigh.

Things are not looking good from the male perspective. Gil had a girlfriend in high school, which makes me think I need a boyfriend, otherwise how is a guy going to know he has to ask me to the prom? I mean, without a boyfriend, I'm throwing caution to the wind, leaving it all to chance. And that is just not me. I don't take chances.

All I know is the closer prom gets, the more pathetic my life becomes and the tighter my parents' grip seems to be. I am desperately close to losing all sense of sanity. Maybe that's too dramatic for four days of effort, but the results? Ugh, the results!

Here's the thing: I don't know that I was all that in touch with my sanity to begin with.

Claire's parents have left for Hawaii, and I've talked

my mother into letting her stay here some of the time. Normally I'd go there and we just wouldn't mention the little "parents on vacation" part—but I'm not really in a place to be caught at the moment because I'm still pursuing the prom date and the blonde highlights.

Oh my gosh, oh my gosh. I have nearly $7,000 saved! Just when I think I can't wear homemade clothes anymore, I check out my bank account and think I totally can! Because the more I save, the quicker I'm on my own and out of this prison my parents call a home. Making my own choices! Blonde highlights, the college of my choice . . . dating. Putting my life on hold may prove to be worth it.

Still, I didn't put my check in the bank. (Once I do that, I have to get my parents' signature to get it out.) I pocketed all the money this week—$168. I feel so guilty, it's almost as if I stole it, but Gil is right. I have to let people know I'm interested in a social life, and I can't do that if I'm dressed like a hostess.

It's time I made some changes. Took some responsibility for myself and forced my parents to see reality. (That's what Claire says anyway.) I'm going to the mall this weekend. I'm going to buy real clothes. Not hand-sewn frocks or apparel from the children's section, deemed appropriate by my mother. No, I'm going to a real store. I'm even going to price cell phones while I'm there. With unlimited texting!

Oh, the prom update. Not much to say there, but after these changes, who knows what can happen?

1. ~~Brian Logan.~~ Improper laying on of hands. On his girlfriend, no less. I'm not the steal-a-man sort.

2. Steve Crisco. It's all review in Calculus so far—hasn't even acknowledged my presence, except with another rousing wave story.

3. ~~Greg Connolly.~~ Like I said, I'm not the steal-your-man type, and Claire's J.Crew style is my only hint here, but it speaks loud and clear. Leave it to my best friend to add on more humiliation.

4. ~~Kelvin Matthews.~~ Dad got laid off—transferred to public school.

5. Chase Doogle. The new and improved Daisy Crispin is coming your way. And I'm going to flirt!

Oh, and I'm grounded. I forgot about a math assignment the first day of school, and my parents saw it at the online parent connect. Heinous technology. But on an up note, it's good from the perfectionist standpoint, right? I failed at something!

❧ 7 ❧

Saturday mornings rock, but this Saturday morning my mind is filled with my first plan of treason: a trip to the mall. I think my mom and dad were looking for my praise about their "show" when I came home from work, but I'd rather wax my head than acknowledge the most humiliating experience of my high school career. Which, for anyone who knows me, is saying something.

I usually get to sleep in—well, at least until eight a.m., when Sergeant Dad comes in and exposits on my laziness, and then I lounge in my jammies, finish homework, and hang out on Facebook while I wait for Claire to wake up.

Today, however, I am awake at the crack of dawn, thinking about how I will sound casual about Claire going shopping and I'm just tagging along. My first genuine lie to my parents, and I would totally feel guilty if I didn't think about Gil's face yesterday, which said it all. If I don't break away now, I will be stuck here with their plan for my life. If my parents had a rundown business like his father's, I'd be slaving away there trying to salvage it. Is that the life I want?

"Daisy!"

I nearly jump out of my skin as my dad pounds on my

door. I stare at the door, taking in Saint Beckham's profile as he studies the soccer ball he's just kicked. "Good mornin', David. I totally think you should dump Posh and take me to the prom." I kick my legs over the side of the bed.

My dad pounds on my door more fervently. "Daisy. Open this door. It's nearly 8:30."

"Criminal," I mumble, making my way to the door.

He's holding a giant garbage bag, which is not an image you want first thing in the morning. It implies work. And I've been working all week! For money. Actual motivation.

"Your mother wants you to come out and help her weed. Get dressed. You're wasting the day. Oh, and Claire's here. You've got five minutes. I assume she knows you're grounded."

Of course she knows. She's usually the reason I am grounded, but it usually feels worth it. I shuffle out into the living room, where I see Claire dressed like a human tent of primary colors.

"What are you doing?" I ask her.

"I got a job."

"What do you mean you got a job? You don't need a job."

"You have a job."

"I have no money."

"It's good for self-respect to have a job. You know that hot-dog stand in the mall?"

"You are not wearing that thing in public. That is not good for anyone's self-respect."

"I totally am. You should have seen my parents' faces, Daisy. I Facebooked my picture, and they got it while boarding the plane. They almost cancelled their trip! I tried to get a job at Nordstrom, but my nails were painted black, and they were all nice, but you could tell they weren't going to hire me."

"Were you wearing your spider nose ring?"

"I was! You think that was it?" Claire shrugs. "So I went to get a lemonade, and then I saw it. I thought, That has to be the most heinous outfit in the entire mall. That's the job I need! It says, Mom and Dad, I need your help."

"No, it says, Dr. Phil, I need your help."

She twirls about. "Can you see me showing up to the club in this? Not only will people think I need a job, but then, to work in the mall! It's so blue-collar."

I lift up my hands. "Hello? I am standing here. Some people need that job, you know. They don't dress like a psychotic circus tent for fun."

"Whatever. You're just jealous."

"Yeah, that's it. You need to get dressed, I'm going shopping today. For real clothes, and you're coming with me." I clap my hands like a seal. "Shopping!"

"No, I'm working," she says with a straight face. "Besides, aren't you grounded?"

"I told my mom I was going to spend some money to buy new pants. She doesn't have time right now to sew up my black ones, so it's a modesty issue."

"Ah."

"Come on, you're going to steal my joy? The one time I need to go to the mall, and you're going to tell me you're busy? You owe me! Go quit your job so someone who actually needs it can have it."

"I can't go shopping. I have to work."

"What's the sudden work ethic about? Are you trying to shame your parents again?" We walk back to my room and I shut the door behind us. "And I'm pricing a cell phone. You don't want to miss that."

"I thought you were already in trouble. If your mother finds a pair of holey jeans or a cell phone in here, it will be like you've left the faith altogether. Have mercy on me. They already think I'm to blame for everything you do wrong."

"You generally are responsible for everything I do wrong. If I'm not with you, I'm working."

"It takes two to tango." Claire pauses. "Who am I kidding? Get dressed. I quit."

My dad is in the doorway, frowning. He opened the door silently. I swear he hovers, just waiting for me to screw up. It's like he enjoys it. "What do you want, Dad?"

"I want you to get up and go help your mother. I have a job today, and your mother needs help in the garden."

"It's my day off," I whine. It's sort of hard to take my dad seriously about a "job" after yesterday's fiasco. He's waiting for me to say something about his performance, but I refuse. I won't give him the satisfaction of telling him he humiliated me. Or that he has no street cred whatsoever when it comes to rapping.

"You're a part of this family. You live under this roof, and as a member of this household, there are chores we ask of you. School comes first, so if work and chores are too much for you, you'll quit your job."

Work is my only respite. There is no way on earth I'm giving up my job. I abhor when my dad lays down the law. It's almost like another persona for him, just one more gig in the dad suit.

"Claire, Daisy is grounded this week."

94

"A week? For not doing one page of homework? Man, that is stiff!"

My dad ignores her comment. "You're welcome to stay here, since I know your parents are gone, but Daisy's had trouble with the truth lately and I want to nip that in the bud. Nothing is more important than character, Daisy. Nothing."

"But . . ." Claire pouts, her lip protruding. She is so good. She actually lets her bottom lip quiver. I have no idea how she does that, but it's a skill I might want to learn. I think if my dad had her acting skills, we would not be living in this dump. "Mr. Crispin, it wasn't Daisy's fault what happened. There were others in Calculus who didn't do the assignment because the teacher hadn't written it down. I'm sure they'll fix it on the computer system on Monday. There wasn't time, being the weekend and all."

"Daisy's nearly an adult, Claire. She needs to be responsible for herself, and she should have asked for homework."

"I wish you could see everyone else's scores. That's what that online system doesn't tell parents. It doesn't tell them when the teachers screw up, only their kids. But I'm willing to bet you real money, Mr. Crispin, that come Monday, I'll be proven right and Daisy's grade will be corrected."

My dad watches Claire carefully. He can't tell if she's telling the truth or not, which says something about his own acting skills. He leans against the doorjamb, ducking his head. My dad has infinitely long legs and a mere scrap of hair on the top of his head, which he tries to round out with oversized mutton-chop sideburns. If there were any Dickens parts around here, he'd be a shoo-in.

"Claire, I think I should speak with your parents about

leaving you alone. You're far too young to be left at your age."

"Well, we have an alarm, you know, and Marisa stays, but she gets so little time with her family. I hate to have her babysit me when her own children need her."

"That's admirable of you. Daisy, why don't you and Claire go get her things? I don't want you staying by yourself, Claire, but this isn't over, Daisy." He walks out of the room and calls behind him, "But enough plotting, you two! If you've taken advantage of someone, God is aware of that!"

I flatten my lips. "Thanks a lot. Let's go before he changes his mind. You are a terrible liar."

"Would it be better if I were a good one?" She shrugs. "I mean, really."

"Did you notice my dad didn't even ask you about your outfit? I'm telling you, Claire, whatever this identity crisis is, it's time to lose it. My dad isn't even responding. You know it's bad when you can't get a rise out of my father. I mean, the man lives to preach."

My dad comes back into view. "I heard that. I wondered what was up with the outfit, Claire."

"I start a new job today. I make lemonade at the mall." She does a little twirl.

"That's very brave of you, I'm proud of you." Dad smirks at me. "You should think about getting a job at the mall, then you wouldn't have to work during the week and take time away from your studies."

It's everything not to roll my eyes. Yeah, I should leave my customer-service job where I create ledgers and Excel spreadsheets for decent money to squish lemons in obscene shorts. There's the future for me. It would not matter what

I did, that man will never be proud of me. There is never a point where he says, "Yeah, that's good."

"All right, I'll see you girls later. Remember, I want you back here to help your mother as soon as you pick up Claire's things."

Sometimes I wonder how my father would react if I really did get into trouble. I take my frustration out on Claire. "You are so bad. Don't you have any guilt? 'It doesn't tell them when the teachers screw up.'"

"I used to have guilt. Your parents used to scare the daylights out of me, but now I just think your dad will never be happy, and it makes me feel violent, actually. Rebellious." Claire looks at herself in the mirror as she talks, and checks out her backside. "Nothing you do is ever good enough, and that totally ticks me off. Like he's perfect. I mean, anyone who hasn't bought a new pair of pants in what, ten years? That is so not perfect. I just get sick of the way he treats you, like you're four and haven't made a good decision in your life."

"His pants? You've got my dad's mutton chops, his lack of solid employment, his rap attempt in front of everyone we know, and you're going to pick on his pants? Claire, that's the least of his problems."

She scowls at the door. "He wants to control everything! Life doesn't work that way."

"All right," I say, trying to calm her down. "He's frugal. He's careful about what he spends."

"No, Daisy. Your dad is cheap. Frugal is spending less for what you want. Your father thinks if he spends anything, all the world will fall apart, and greater humanity depends upon his skill to be cheap. That, dear Daisy, is cheap and strange. My parents may spend like water, but sheesh, they're not afraid to live their lives." She picks up my hairbrush and starts to brush her hair. "Got any spray gel?"

"Stop it," I tell her, grabbing my brush. "You're not going to work. You're helping me shop. You obviously need to work some anger out."

"You've waited this long, what's another week? Your dad's done it his whole life."

My first inclination is to support my dad. I mean, it's hard to hear Claire's assessment of him. Harsh. But when he comes back down the hallway, he's wearing his pirate pants and puffy shirt, and it's sort of hard to defend him. He's also accessorized with a fake, sagging parrot doll on his shoulder. It's not exactly the stuff of pride, is it?

Claire turns to me and rolls her eyes. "Your dad thinks what I'm wearing to work is weird? I'm seventeen. What about him?"

"Shh," I hiss back at her. "You're not helping."

We run out to Claire's car and I call to my mom, "Bye, see ya when I get back. We'll help you with the garden then. Dad said it was okay to go get Claire's stuff. By the way, you look great today, Mom. Gardening is your look, girlfriend." I stumble into the car before she has a chance to say another living thing or place another hard-and-fast rule on my day. I breathe out extensively as Claire pulls out of the driveway. "We made it."

She looks at my legs. "Sort of. You're wearing your pajamas."

I look down. "I totally am. Go back. No, wait." I look back at my mother, who is bent over her flower bed, watching us. "Don't. I'll borrow something at your house."

Claire is about five inches shorter than me, but I ignore this fact. It's that, or my mother.

My mom yells, "Daisy!"

"Just go, just go," I tell Claire.

"Daisy, stop right there!"

Claire lets the car idle. Mom saunters over with a hoe in her hand and leans on it. She's wearing blue-jean overalls and a long-sleeved plaid shirt. She reaches into her pocket and pulls out a wad of cash. "Here. It's for your shopping trip."

"How'd you—What's this?"

"You were right. You are the only one who dresses the way you do at your school, and that has to be hard."

And it's not helped by my parents' Donny and Marie rapping onstage. "Yeah?"

"Go to the mall and get yourself some clothes." Mom doesn't meet my eyes. "I heard you and Claire through the heating vent."

"Where'd you get this?"

"I earned it. Don't worry, it's mine."

"Not doing that rap yesterday?" I don't want tainted money.

She smiles and leans in to talk to Claire. "Shop at affordable stores, Claire. Daisy's dad isn't a high-profile lawyer."

Maybe the pirate suit gave that away.

"We will. We totally will," Claire says.

Claire and I look at one another. "Mom? What about Dad?" I ask.

"I'll take care of that. Go shop," my mother says as she pulls her gardening gloves from under her arm and studies her approach.

I squeeze my head under the windshield and look up.

"What are you doing?"

"Jesus is coming back. It's the only possible explanation."

99

Claire roars her engine to life and pulls away from the curb. She stares at my pajamas. "Why didn't you go back in and change?"

"Just go. By the way, I told you my father wasn't cheap." I cross my arms in front of my chest.

"Your mother gave you the money."

"Well, where'd she get it, Miss Smarty Pants?"

"Not from your father, I know that much. You really should go change. What are you going to borrow from me, a night-gown?" Claire asks as we drive away.

"Shorts. A skirt, I don't know, just let's go. If we go back, you know I'm not getting out again. My real mom will return, and I can't take that chance. This is the first day of my new life!" I fumble through her glove compartment, tossing CDs on the floor and flipping through useless paperwork. "Where's your makeup? You always have makeup in here."

"I'm trying to be more organized. Besides, I told you, I had to work, so I already put it on at home. I gave you makeup four days ago. Where is it?"

"It wouldn't fit in my wristlet," I say sheepishly.

"Priorities, Daisy. I'm supposed to be at the store at ten for training. We open at eleven today, so I'm glad to take you to the mall, but I can't shop. You can drop by the store and show me what you've bought."

I gaze at my friend, who is literally a stranger to me right now. Getting organized? In a hurry to get to work? "What is wrong with you? I let the spider ring go, but this—you're self-starting now? Has the earth shifted? I want my best friend back. The fun, flaky one."

"Daisy, you know, if your dad was remotely reasonable, I wouldn't have to break you out at 8:30 on a Saturday morning. You said you want this year to be different, but how can that happen if you do things exactly the same? If you want a different result, the only person you can change is you."

"Who *are* you?"

"My life coach said I can be whomever I like. I can dress in a poetic mood, but I need to be adaptable and work within the world's boundaries. No one wants to hire me if my looks scare them, but the truth is, I was only dressing that way for Ryan Embers, and he never noticed me. It turns out I'm not very good at dark poetry either. I'm too happy."

"I think it's hard to be dark when you drive a convertible Mustang and have a life coach at seventeen. What the heck is a life coach anyway?"

"My mom hired her. She's amazing. She said I could act like I didn't care about all those kids at school, but then if I did care, I wasn't being honest with myself. It's better to be honest and deal with the pain. If it hurts, deal with it. Otherwise you start doing crap like cutting or drinking to deal with the pain." She shrugs.

"Your mom is afraid you're going to cut?"

"I think my goth phase started that fear."

"Claire, I think your parents need to spend less time on vacation and more time with you."

She stops at the stop sign. "My parents aren't on vacation."

"They're home?"

"No, my dad's in New York on business and my mom is in Hawaii at a spa."

"But you said—"

"I lied."

"Why?"

"My dad's left us."

I actually laugh. "That's not funny."

"I'm not joking," she says.

"You kept this secret from me? Claire, I could forgive the nose piercing, but this—you don't just handle this stuff yourself." I allow her words to sink in, and I feel the pain she's avoiding. My head throbs. "Is that why you're so ticked at my dad today?"

"No, I'm ticked at your dad because he treats you like a toddler. I'm ticked at *my* dad because he's avoiding me. Keeps giving me these excuses, how I don't understand. That it's between him and my mom, but how is that true? She's not home! He left me!"

"He hasn't, Claire. He gives you everything to make your life perfect. Remember at the club when we bought everyone at the pool a round of Cokes, and he just laughed it off and paid the bill?"

"How many times have you been around my dad? In all the years you've been my best friend, have you ever spent the night when he was home?"

I'm awestruck at the obvious. "No. He travels a lot, though. Some men have to do that."

"My parents don't care what I do, Daisy. We may be invisible at school, but at least you're not invisible at home too."

"So that's what the circus-tent shorts are about. Claire, your dad's your dad. If your parents are splitting up, he's not going to abandon you financially—"

"He told her we were holding him back. We. He's not leaving my mother. He's leaving us. And I don't want his money!"

"It sucks to work. Haven't I mentioned that? It's not cute to answer to a boss when you have no choice. It's not fun to work overtime because the company is in need of your skills." I slam her glove compartment shut. "Did the life coach say that was a good way to deal with the pain? Just go shopping like a normal rich girl!"

Claire's face changes, and it dawns on me that maybe my friend isn't as tough as I thought. "Shopping doesn't work anymore."

"Why is your mom in Hawaii?"

"She doesn't know Marisa quit."

"Marisa quit? Claire, you've been staying totally alone?"

"They're arguing over the house."

"*Who* is arguing over the house? Marisa?"

"No, my parents. Marisa doesn't want to be stuck in the battles anymore, so she quit. My dad would call her and tell her one thing, then my mother would call back and say the opposite." Claire half laughs. "It's cool that she can do that, just quit. I'm stuck."

"You have to tell your mother she's gone."

"She wouldn't believe it because that would interfere with her life. Right now the only thing that would concern her is if her wine glass was empty."

My mouth is hanging wide open. I keep waiting for Claire to say, "Psych!" and this crazy story will be over. Claire has everything. Claire has parents caught up in their own love affair. "I've seen your parents. They're crazy about each other."

"Until things go wrong, then they're just crazy. They turn on each other like two Dobermans set loose in a ring. The things they've said to each other . . ." She shakes her head, clutching the steering wheel. "I couldn't even repeat it, and you know me, I'd say anything."

"I feel horrible you've been keeping this all to yourself."

"You've got enough troubles."

"Bad fashion sense is hardly having your world ripped apart."

"I don't know, you do bad fashion sense pretty well." She laughs.

"When's your mom coming back?"

"I don't know. She thinks my dad is there. He thinks she's there, so neither one of them is in a hurry. Apparently they need to be apart for the separation to officially start, so they're both sticking their feet in the sand. My mother more literally."

"Aren't they at least calling to check up on you?"

"Sure, but they ask how things are, I tell them fine, and that's it." Claire gets a twinkle in her eye. The one that always gets me into trouble. "So since they're both gone and this is our senior year, I think we should throw a party. The kind of party that kids will talk about at our reunion."

"A party? Claire, your mother isn't going to stay in Hawaii forever."

Claire shrugs.

"You have to tell her about Marisa so she knows you're alone."

"Do I?"

"What about your dad? We'll never get away with this. We're not the types to throw parties, remember? First off, who would come?"

"My dad's doing a teaching stint at New York University. He won't be back until after the holidays. If he comes back at all. My mom seems to think he'll find a twentysomething student and won't come back. In the meantime, she's drowning herself in Botox and hot rock massages on a Hawaiian beach."

"Your dad's coming back. Stop that. You cannot stay home alone for over a month."

"You know, I was thinking of a party where we invite everyone from school."

"Forget about your parents, my father would kill us," I say with the inflection of "duh" in my voice. "I have to tell them you're here alone."

"Don't you dare! Daisy Crispin, if you tell your parents about mine, I'll . . . think of something."

Which is worse than if she'd come up with revenge on the fly. If Claire has time to think about it, there's no telling what I'd be up against.

"Your dad would be upset, Daisy." She taps her finger on her chin. "If he found out about it, Chase might have to find out who sent him those secret admirer roses every Valentine's Day since fourth grade."

"You wouldn't dare!"

"Worse yet, if your dad did find out, he'd come to school and put on a play about it. Do you really think you're up for that kind of humiliation senior year?"

"Claire, if our friendship means anything to you, you cannot tell Chase a thing. I can't take that kind of humiliation. I'm going to prom this year."

"You? Going to prom?" Claire starts to cackle. "Why would you want to go to prom?"

"What are you, the wicked stepsister? Yes, me going to prom. Why is that so ridiculous? Most girls want to go to prom."

"Sorry, I thought you were joking." She slows to face me

and puts her colorful beanie on her head. "A party would give you a chance to spend time with Chase. Real time. Not the kind where Amber walks in and projectile vomits on you, or whatever she's going to do for attention. Because we wouldn't invite her. In fact, we'd uninvite her."

Suddenly I don't feel so goody-two-shoes. Or even remotely perfectionist, except about the party planning.

"A party would make us matter. Think about it, Daisy. The pool house out back. If my parents divorce, how long do you think we'll have that?"

"A lot of kids can do a lot of damage."

"We wouldn't even have to let them in the house, and we would go down in history for having the most rockin' party that St. James Academy has ever seen. 'Class of 2011,' they'll say. 'Now that was the year to be here.'"

"Christians have a phrase for *karma*, right? It's called reaping what you sow. We already sow a lot of misery. What if we make it worse for ourselves?" I try to force the thoughts of my lies out of my head for the moment.

Claire raises her arm toward the distance. "Think about it. We could have *Gossip Girl* playing on the big screen outside. We could buy party supplies with my credit card. My parents would never know I bought eighty gallons of soda until after the fact."

"We could pay cash for the supplies. We don't have to add stealing to the mix."

"We could personally uninvite Amber and Britney, and then that would be the last we'd have to worry about them. My mom told me that all the girls who are so beautiful and developed in high school will be fat and fake blonde by the reunion."

"I can't imagine your mother saying that." But yeah, really I can. Claire's mother is gorgeous. I've told Claire that if they ever do *The Real Housewives of Silicon Valley*, her mother has to star in the cast. She would make the current housewives appear tame.

The reality of Claire's parents splitting strikes me. "We can't do this to your parents, Claire. They've got to be under a lot of pressure." My parents may be deranged, but at least they're deranged together.

"So I guess you don't really want to go to prom then. How's Chase going to even ask you? At school, Amber stalks him, and at home, you can't even use the phone."

"He can Facebook me."

"How romantic. Maybe when he asks you to marry him, he can tweet it."

"Claire." I snap my waistband on my flamingo jammies. "Gil says we should let a guy know how we feel. We can do that without a party. We should at least try it first. Do you have someone you're crushing on? Maybe if we focus on that"—I swallow hard—"and not the party, and pray . . . you know, your parents' thing will work itself out."

"Gil? Since when do you listen to Gil?"

"Since he was popular and we're not."

She nods. "But when was he popular? 1960?"

"He graduated in 2004. He's not that ancient."

"He does look like Josh Lucas," she reasons.

"There's that."

"But if Gil's wrong, we've made complete idiots out of ourselves for nothing."

"No!" I raise my finger. "Then we know the guy wasn't that into us."

"Why do I want to know that?" Claire asks. "Ignorance is bliss."

"So we're done with the party idea?"

"I didn't say that, just that I'll reconsider if shopping does the trick and brings back the thrill of the hunt. Regarding the party? You owe me, Daisy. I've put up with your second-grade schedule for twelve years. You'll be leaving home in less than a year. It's the party or I give up."

"That's blackmail. But I want to come back home at some point, not be unwelcome to return!"

Claire pulls into the parking lot of the mall. "There are gym pants in the back. Go ahead and change."

I climb into the backseat and pull out her gym bag, which reeks. "These are foul."

"Well, yeah. I was taking them home to get cleaned. Just get dressed so we can go explain to my manager why I can't work."

"I'm going to have a plume of stench following me!"

"Then wear your pajamas. They're cute. Certainly no uglier than your regular outfits."

I stick my tongue out and yank off my jammies. I pick up the hardened gym shorts. They've morphed into an unforgiving shape. "I can't do it."

"You are such a baby."

"What are *you* going to wear? Won't they want their uniform back when you tell them you're not working?"

"I'll work that out," Claire says.

As I shimmy back into my jammies, I'm struck by all Claire has kept inside about her parents, and my thoughts come tumbling out. "Are you testing how gullible I am again? I've never even seen your parents raise their voices. Not once."

"My parents should be the actors. They've got a lot more experience than your parents. I don't think anyone but me has ever seen them fight, and trust me, it is not pretty."

"What's one party?" I ask her. "I mean, in the scheme of things, we've been good kids."

"I know, right?"

We both look at each other and break into laughter. Before this, the new Daisy was nothing more than a dream. Today the dream takes shape. Even as my conscience sears me with guilt.

8

I feel this surge of electricity as I enter the mall, much like when I'm in Chase's presence. My endorphins are flowing and sparkling all over the place like fireworks. I'm going shopping! Even in my dorky pajamas, which I have to say seem as though I planned the look, I'm SpongeBob-happy.

"My endorphins are going crazy. I'm euphoric. I'm stupid-happy."

"Okay . . ." Claire stops abruptly in front of the kiddie carts for hire and shakes her head. "You know, it's not the numbers."

"What's not the numbers?"

"All this time, everyone said, 'Daisy is so good with numbers. She's brilliant with numbers.'"

"Am I missing something?"

"Naturally, you want to major in finance because you're good with numbers, right?"

"And living on nothing," I remind her. "Cheap is a fine art, and I am Michelangelo."

"But you have just as many facts about sloths, endorphins, neurotoxins. Pretty much anything geeky."

110

"That was my father," Max says. "We're from Argentina."
Claire looks at me, and I can't help but laugh.

"It's in South America," I tell her and look back at Max.
"She's not racist, just geographically challenged. We were
friends with Angie Chen for three years before Claire real-
ized Chinese wasn't a language." Max blinks. "Usually, it's
Mandarin or Cantonese," I explain to Max, as I once did
to Claire.

"Isn't South America where Mexico is?" Claire asks, as
though (1) Max can't hear her, or (2) I might have a useless
fact mixed up. Both of which are impossible.

"Mexico is Central America," Max says. "Close." He grins.
"Well, not really. Mexico's in the Northern Hemisphere, we're
in the Southern. Some of my country is close to Antarctica."

"What is with you people and hemispheres? Who talks like
that? I know Antarctica. Where the big penguins are!" Claire
offers. "I saw *Penguins*." She turns to me. "Daisy, did you hear
that? He knows his hemispheres too. I cannot believe I have
said that word twice in a day. Do you see what you're doing
to the good people of Silicon Valley?"

"You're from Buenos Aires?" I'm staying pressed against
the counter so that Max won't notice I'm dressed like a street
person in my jammies.

"Recoleta. We lived right by the famous cemetery where
Eva Peron is buried. It's the French section of town—that's
why I speak French."

"Don't cry for me, Argentina!" Claire says. "My parents
made me sit through that play in London. It wasn't my
favorite."

"You saw a play in London," I mumble. "Let me do the
complaining here."

"Did you know sloths move so slowly that algae can grow
on their fur?"

"See!" She points at me. "You can't major in finance, Daisy.
You have to do something in the sciences. That's where your
heart is."

"My dad says it's too hard to make money in that. We
talked about neuroscience."

"And yet your dad puts on puppet shows and your family's
all here. You're eating and going to private school. My parents
are on two different sides of the hemisphere—"

"Actually, New York and Hawaii are both in the Northern
Hemisphere. Oh, and the Western too. They're in the same
hemisphere."

"Enough, Daisy. If you drop one of your stupid facts at the
party, our chances of being remembered for the greatest party
ever are over. I'm only telling you about science because I think
your career is headed the wrong direction. The clothes are
the tip of the iceberg. You keep trying to make your parents
happy, and you never think about what you want."

"The sloth fact totally makes sense," I say. I'm not going to
let her simply tell me I'm crazy. "I was thinking of the energy
that spiked when I walked in the mall with the hope that I'd
be dressed differently on Monday, and it went together. The
sloth extending so little energy."

"It doesn't go together. You have to speak the whole sen-
tence, Daisy, not just half of it, or you don't make any sense.
Not that your facts make any sense to the rest of us. We are
not listing facts today. You are not Spock. At least try for
Uhura and be hot, all right? You are not the History Channel
or Animal Planet, and you are not an accountant, so change
your major!" Claire catches her breath before starting up

again. "We're shopping. If you would like to offer up a fact about a great purchase, I'm all ears, but if you have anything to say about the two-toed sloth or how many hemispheres may in fact exist, I don't want to hear about it."

"I read it in a novel."

"And? That's half a thought."

"I read about the sloth in a novel." I spin my wristlet around.

She stops the motion. "I'm not getting through. All right, what are you nervous about? Is it the idea we might throw a party and Chase might come?"

"What if I buy the wrong clothes? Worse yet, what if they make the wrong impression? Or no impression? What if it's our party and no one talks to me?"

"Your parents took care of the 'no impression' yesterday. You're covered there. People will talk to us or we'll kick them out. I'm totally hiring a bouncer. He's going to look like Chris Brown, and if anyone messes with us, I'm saying, 'Do you want him to go all Chris Brown on you? He will, so get out!'" Claire shakes out her hair and lets out a deep breath. "Let's focus. Clothes are about how you feel. You find clothes that you feel great in, and that emanates from every pore. So you give off this great energy. Great energy, magnetic presence with guys. It's simple math, so even you ought to understand that."

I don't want to put too much faith in a new pair of jeans. Chances are, I'll go back to school on Monday as the same dork who left on Friday.

"I've got to go quit and tell them I'll turn in my uniform when the stores open. You want to come?"

"I wouldn't miss it!"

The neon lights of the food court are dark, and the only noise is a song with differing languages. "I wonder if a food court really is supposed to be this international. Like, I wonder if in Topeka, you hear all these languages."

Claire glares at me.

"Sorry." Behind the bleached countertop at the hot-dog stand is some poor guy in a horizontal-striped shirt with unfortunate red pants—less intrusive than Claire's full spectrum of primary colors, but certainly not masculine in any way, shape, or form. "That is just wrong," I whisper to Claire. Not only does he have to dress like that, today he has to do it alone. "Tsk tsk. I'll just wait over here."

"Daisy?" The guy in the bad outfit stands up, and I freeze. Max Diaz is wrestling with a Lucite container of lemons and ice. He stops what he's doing and wipes his hands on a towel. Oh my goodness, I think I'm speaking Spanish in my head.

"*Muy guapo. Caliente.*" I fan my face. "He makes that ridiculous outfit look good."

"Thanks," he says. His gorgeous olive skin turns crimson. So apparently I did say that out loud.

"You took French," Claire says to me.

"I speak French too. I lived in the French section of Buenos Aires." He stares at Claire in her matching obnoxious uniform. "You're who I'm training today?"

"Well, actually, I came to tell you—"

"She's here reporting for duty, Max." I give him a salute.

"*You* need a job?" he asks Claire, who clearly, with her salon highlights and professional manicure, does not look the part of corn-dog queen.

"Yeah, I hired on with a Mexican manager yesterday. Juan somebody. He said to be here at ten."

Claire starts speaking loudly. "So what kind of houses do you have there? Tin roofs? Grass huts? Was it weird to get running water?"

The back of his jaw twitches on both sides. "We have French-inspired buildings. Buenos Aires is called the Paris of South America. About thirteen million people in the city and surrounding areas. Makes San Jose look like a paltry suburb."

"Oh, so, like, you have indoor plumbing."

"Yes, Claire. I think we might even be able to impress you there."

I like how he's not offended by Claire's blatant ignorance. He's very gentle with her, and his kindness endears me to him. The fact that he speaks three languages and knows what hemisphere he lives in doesn't hurt either. Nor does the fact that he's talking to me, plain and simple.

He steps down off the platform and comes beside me. He takes a look at my pink and green pajamas, smiles slightly, then grabs my waist and hand. "We are famous for the tango." He starts to dance me around the food court. "Which is not only a dance but a style of music too. Did you hear that, Claire? A style of music," he shouts over my shoulder. "We have ice cream delivery bikes to offer you a *limon* when you're parched."

I'm so lost in the movement, I forget what I'm wearing until I see Max focus on my legs. "I—uh—"

"Nice pants." His eyes twinkle, and right then I think I'm in love because Max seems to find it charming that I'm in sleepwear. Chase who?

Claire sticks her head between us, and Max pulls away. "So, Max, Daisy and I were talking about the party we're going to give. Maybe right after Halloween or so. Kind of an All Saints' Day party. Do you know any good bands that we might get to play?"

"Bands?" I never said I'd go along with this.

"Bands?" Max asks.

I pull him away by the arm. "Never mind. We don't need any bands." I glare at Claire, then turn back to Max. "So if Buenos Aires is so fabulous, why come here?" I don't make mention of the bad hot-dog suit. I figure he must have his reasons, and who am I to judge?

He says something back to me, but it's like a one-sided tennis volley. I've lost sight of what he's saying. I'm mesmerized by both his intellect and his gorgeous bone structure. He hops back onto the hot-dog platform and starts fiddling with the cash register.

"You should be a model," I tell him dreamily.

Claire has her lip upturned, but I ignore her.

"So is it like Rio? I've always wanted to go there after seeing the *Christ the Redeemer* sculpture in the modern seven wonders of the world."

"It's better than Rio. More sophisticated. I think you'd prefer the educated porteños to the club scene in Rio."

I'm lost in his eyes, and in the idea of international travel. "I would love to go anywhere. Claire's been to Europe."

"I'm going back next year," Max says. "For college. The University of Argentina is one of the best in the world. And it's free."

"Free?" My ears perk up. "For Argentians?"

"Argentines," he corrects me. "And foreigners. You'd have to complete your compulsories and take up residence. But that only takes a year, and the University of Buenos Aires has one of the best reputations in the world."

"Get that look off your face," Claire says to me. "You are not going to Argentina. Listen to your best friend. Switching from accounting to science, that's your deal. That's all you have to think of right now besides the party. You are not going to a foreign country. You have to master this one first."

"Finance, not accounting. Completely different majors."

"Whatever. Can we go?"

Max ignores Claire—and I like him for that too. Knowing when to ignore Claire is a gift. "Science?" Max says. "The university has won many Nobel Prizes in science."

For a moment, I allow myself to dream about attending school in a different country. The idea glistens in my brain, like new numbers not found yet.

Claire comes around and pulls Max by the arm, apparently forgetting her role as an employee. "Look, Don Juan, this girl is ripe for your romanticized version of South America, where the education is free and the clothing is optional. Let's get to work, shall we?" She looks back over her shoulder. "Daisy, you go shopping. I'm going to learn how to stomp lemons." She crosses her arms and waits for Max's full attention, but blissfully, he's still looking at me, and I'm seeing our future. He's teaching at the university. I'm teaching English to the other young mothers.

At that point, it registers that Claire isn't coming shopping with me.

"I thought—" I pull away from Max. "I thought you weren't working. You were going to quit, remember?"

"Here are my keys so you can leave when you're done. Just come back and get me at—what time, Don?" she shouts at Max.

He ignores her barb. "Come back at six. The rush will be

over by then, and I can close down alone." Max looks at me again. "I meant to tell you, it's smart of you to wear pajamas shopping. So much easier to try things on, it's a wonder no one's thought of it before."

I brush my fingertips on my collar. "Well, you know—"

Claire pushes me away from the hot-dog stand. "Look." She blocks my view of Max and forces me back with her staccato words. "How does someone from the French section of Argentina go to a public high school in San Jose and end up at St. James while running his father's hot-dog cart? Do the math, Daisy. Guys don't come from Buenos Aires to run hot-dog joints. This guy is a player, and you're putty in his well-practiced hands. Now go, shop and stay away from here. Max is not invited to our party."

I have to keep reminding myself that this is my best friend and she only wants what's best for me. Otherwise it may result in physical pain for her.

Prom Journal
September 22
166 Days until Prom
Fact of the Day: Your legs get sticky working with lemonade all day. Somehow I thought after our first-grade lemonade stand at the corner, Claire and I were done with that avenue of high finance. Claire was like a giant piece of cotton candy when she finished working.

Life is a mess! Claire stayed over the weekend, but she said nothing about her parents both being gone and the maid not

118

being there. I know my mother would have called Claire's mother and ratted her out. Then I'd be off the hook. I hate the thought of her rattling around in that big house alone at night. I'm not so much worried about her safety as how completely comfortable she is without anyone around. She calls up the grocer, orders weekly deliveries like she's been doing it her whole life, and then signs the slip without thought to who pays the bill—and someone must, or they wouldn't keep delivering.

Right now, her only friends are "Gossip Girl" and Rory Gilmore when reruns of "Gilmore Girls" are on. Which, with the size of Claire's satellite dish, is way too often. I tell you, she probably gets television programming from Mars!

This totally surprised me: Claire's still working at the lemonade shack, and she loves it! The second day Claire worked, Amber Richardson came by and recorded her on a cell phone.

Claire took it as her fifteen minutes and totally started dancing. Amber, evil as she is, uploaded the video to You-Tube. But remember, you cannot embarrass Claire. Claire herself downloaded the video and added Beyoncé music, and only then was it obvious she was doing the "Single Ladies" dance. Justin Timberlake on SNL has nothing on my BFF in her Hot Dog on a Stick uniform. Her version went viral, and she became a star at St. James.

Amber tried to tell everyone she did it. She thought of it, but her desperate cries for attention went unheeded. (Oh, and if you're wondering why my prom journal is filled with useless facts about other people and not myself, it's because I have absolutely nothing to report on prom, a prom date, or the male population in general.)

Claire used her dance as her platform to talk about the hugest party of the season—ours (until our parents find out and have us burned at the stake). Claire tweeted for everyone to see that unless she got a personal apology online for all the mean stuff Amber's done to us, Amber would not be invited! I still cannot believe we're going through with this.

The thing is, Amber did apologize, and now we have to invite her bony self or we look like the jerks. I'm so glad I'm dressed decently for the newfound popularity. I went to PacSun for all my school gear. My mother doesn't know it exists, and therefore it is not on the forbidden list. Woo-hoo!!

Here's the thing about flying high that Amber might want to take into account now that she's one of us. It's our nature as the invisible kids to wait to come crashing back to earth. Most days at school, we are on shaky ground at best, but Sarika, Angie, Claire, and me? We ate on the other side of the popular equator for once in our lives, and unlike the fourth grade where nothing was dif-

120

ferent, this experience rocked my world! Chase Doogle and a cold Fizzy Izze in a can? It doesn't get any better than that. I used to be jealous of Amber, and my mom would say there was nothing there to envy—but now I know the truth!

Nothing on prom to report, but the party of the year is in the works, and that's D-day. I will have a date and/or a boyfriend. His name is, and has always been, Chase Doogle.

9

Claire is still preening from her newfound fame of going viral and actually asks me to go with her to youth group. It's a miracle, I tell you, and it takes her mind off her parents' drama, so I'm more than happy to comply. And let's face it, Chase will be there, so she didn't exactly have to twist my arm.

We approach the church gym. The lights are on, the low murmur of excited voices is bursting within, and echoes bounce off the shiny wood floor. Claire turns back from the gym, her usual vigor gone. "Nothing changes here. Youth group is just another venue for taunting."

"Stop it, you're not being taunted anymore. Remember? 'If you liked it, then you should have put a ring on it.'" I do a little dance.

"Don't do that. It's disturbing."

"Come on, what are you waiting for? You're the one who wanted to come."

"I changed my mind," Claire says.

"What's gotten into you?"

"I just don't feel like it all of a sudden."

I think of Chase behind the two sets of doors. "Too bad," I say without a whole lot of compassion. "We're here."

Claire withers in a way that isn't like her at all. She's dressed like a girl. In a simple sundress. Her hair is now a soft, light auburn with professional blonde streaks, and she's wearing mascara. Mascara! Suddenly everything has changed.

"You've got a crush on someone!"

"A what? Oh, get real."

"You're wearing mascara!" I point at her.

"They're fake lashes."

"You're totally crushin' then. Who is it?"

"I'm not crushing. My mother bought fake eyelashes that came with rhinestones at the end, and I used the extra ones in the package."

"You sound so reasonable when you say that."

"Can we go now?" Claire is backing away.

My smile wanes. "You're serious?" Truthfully, I'm glad Claire's here. I'm worried about her, and I think having a bit of prayer will do her good. I want her to tell the truth about her parents so she can get some support. She's keeping their secret, though, and I'm worried it's taking a toll on the lighthearted person she is. "Maybe you'll have some kind of epiphany here and God will speak to you in a way he never has before."

"Or flying monkeys could appear. God's hardly interested in me."

"He listens to me, and he knows I have nothing important to say. Just give it a try tonight. For me? I'm risking everything for your harebrained party idea." I push her gently into the church's gymnasium and she doesn't fight me. If it's the size of the fight in the dog, I'd be the loser for certain—Claire has more fight in her little finger alone.

"You're bringing your backpack inside?" Claire asks me. "No one believes you're going to do any homework. Just leave it in the car. It's like your security blanket."

"If you get cold, I have a sweater. If you have dry lips, I've got gloss. If you shake hands with someone who has a cold, I have antibacterial. I am totally prepared with my backpack."

"Great, if there's a nuclear war tonight, my best friend has a diaper bag for me."

As we enter the gym, the squeak of basketball shoes echoes off the barren walls and the stench of dirty socks fills my nostrils. Guys huddle in the center of the court with a ball, fighting over it like it's the last round object on earth. Secretly they're hoping the girls are drooling over their fancy moves, and every once in a while I catch one of them looking our way to see if we've noticed. I scan the crowd of guys, wondering who might have caught Claire's attention. Granted, I've had hints it could be Greg, but I can't go there since he's on my list of prom backups and we've never liked the same sorts of guys in the past.

Claire has had a boyfriend before. Sean Kendrick. She met him at the country club, and the one thing I remember about him most vividly is that he wore a trench coat 24/7—which of course made me think *flasher*. They broke up when her Christian values got in the way, but she never seemed to care whether he was at her side or he wasn't.

Claire flips her bobbed hair. "Why are girls always relegated to being cheerleaders? Maybe I want to play ball too. Do they ever think of that?" Claire thins her eyes. "Besides, I don't like cheerleaders very much. They're too happy for me."

"There's always an athletic girl out there. Go ahead if

you want to play," I tell her, wondering what on earth she's really trying to say. "What is up with you? Is it a guy? Your parents? What?"

"It's simple. Do you want to know why there are no girls out there? Guys don't fall for girls who can slam them on the court. No guy wants to be schooled by a girl in front of his friends. No guy. I could school most any of these losers, and most of the girls are smart enough to know this, so they choose not to play. They choose to sit here on the sidelines and cheer." She walks toward the open door.

I step away from the basketball court. "Claire!"

She zips away from the door and walks to the girls on the "A" team—and I'm not talking grades here.

"This side of the gym seems more dangerous." I nod toward the circle of popular girls, with their long legs, full figures, and lengthy tresses with salon highlights. Truthfully, Claire could be one of them if she wanted to, and I'm left to wonder if that's what's happening. Is she tired of having me stuck to the bottom of her shoe? Am I bringing her down?

The popular girls are preening in a competition all their own, and it's rougher than what we're seeing on the basketball court. Sure, it resembles a Miss America pageant and not an aerobic sport, but it's far more cutthroat. Don't let the frilly peasant blouses, skinny jeans, and heels fool you.

We're split into several cliques courtside. In fact, we could be numbered by rank: (1) tall, buxom, and gorgeous; (2) buxom and attractive; (3) buxom; (4) skinny and us.

Sometimes I think India's caste system is alive and well in youth groups across America and Sarika has an advantage over all of us. Since she doesn't go to First Union, I can't make this assessment with her, but I bet she wouldn't argue with me.

Claire and I sit on a threadbare sofa pushed up into the corner, and we're able to watch as though invisible—which I guess we are in many ways. I usually have too much homework to come to youth group, but I want to finish a conversation with Chase. I need closure.

"You know, it's been a year since I've come, and not a thing has changed," Claire says as she scans the room with me. "Amber, Britney, and Rachel will try to make my life miserable in overtime. It's like giving them a free gift with purchase. I have to endure these people all day. Why would I want to spend my free time with them?"

"Maybe we should try something different with them. Kill them with kindness," I suggest.

"Or just kill them," Claire says. She brushes her russet-colored bob out of her face. "A tiger doesn't change its stripes with a change of venue. When I'm an actor, they'll be nothing more than a speck on my historical timeline." She says this with all the flair of a Shakespearian lead. Claire's always most comfortable in a role that is not her.

"A night at youth group isn't going to kill you. If you hope to infiltrate Hollywood, it will do you good to play dress-up and pretend. What is high school but one giant rehearsal?"

"Hollywood," she spits. "I'm going to New York. The stage! Why would I waste my talent on the masses? Genuine theater isn't like *High School Musical*. Hollywood is nothing more than a continuation of this popularity contest, but to be on stage . . ." She waves her hand in the distance. "Either in the West End or on Broadway, that is the pinnacle of success. That's where the real thespians stand apart from their peers."

"Whatever. If you end up doing kids' parties like my dad, I will hurt you."

"Max seems to think we're much more sophisticated than the other girls at school. Don't you love that word? *Sophisticated*." She pats her finger on her bottom lip. "We're school nerds, but on the world stage, maybe we're too sophisticated for this one-horse town."

"Yeah, that's it," I say. "I thought you didn't like Max."

"I never said I didn't like him, I said I thought he was a player. But if he's international and he sees us as more sophisticated than, say, Amber Richardson, shouldn't we take that to heart? He would know better than us. All I'm sayin'."

"I thought maybe you decided to come because Greg is here."

She settles deeper into the sofa and stares me down. "Greg! This is about Chase, right?"

Even his name causes my stomach to flutter. "Not entirely. I could use a little group Bible study."

Claire's got that look of pity on her face.

"Don't look at me like that."

"Just leave Chase alone, Daisy. He'll be gone to the Air Force Academy and out of your life anyway. He's a poseur."

"Really? That's how you're going to support me? First, when Max says something nice to me, he's a player, and now Chase is a poseur? Is there someone not ending in 'er' who I might date according to your rigorous standards?"

"Chase needs to stay on the straight and narrow. Greg told me the standards at the academy are really high; that's why he took all the heat that day for starting the fire in wood shop."

"He did start the fire!"

She rolls her eyes. "Let's not discuss it. There's an entire school full of guys. If something was going to happen with you and Chase, don't you think it would have happened by now?"

"Greg's here," I say, feeling betrayed. "I'm just your henchman, is that it? You haven't come here for a year, after all."

Then I see her catch Greg's eye, and neither one of them looks away for what feels like an eternity. He's in her drama class, and they share a love of ye olde English and New York University. But I'm concerned about Greg's love of drama and firearms combined.

"You never thought Chase was out of my league before."

"Greg and I are both trying for the lead in this year's musical. It's *The Phantom of the Opera*, did I tell you?" She doesn't take her eyes off Greg. "Wouldn't he make an amazing phantom?"

"I guess." I don't know what's more disturbing—acerbic, hopeless Claire, or cloudy Claire with a possible chance of a boyfriend.

She bats her eyes. "Don't change the subject."

I clamp my teeth together. "Claire, why do you think prom is so stupid? Why are you past high school already? We're not out of it yet."

She stops and I can see her breathe. "I guess I'm just past it. I'm ready to move on. It feels like the same life day in and day out. I'm ready for a change." Her expression changes to worry, and her forehead crinkles in ways that Renee Zellweger would covet. "Don't tell anyone about Greg Connolly, all right? He's got a lot going on right now, and the last thing he needs to worry about is us."

"What would I tell them? You haven't admitted a thing, other than the fact that you do in fact own an iron for that crisp J.Crew collar. If he's your boyfriend, he should own it."

She sighs. That's the thing about Claire. Once you think you know her, she'll surprise you with some new aspect about her. The only consistency is her ability to be inconsistent.

For the most part, Claire and I haven't shared on guys. Mostly because there's nothing to report and it's too humiliating to admit. But seeing the frown on her face, I unzip my backpack and pull out my frilly pink prom journal. She might be above it all, but I'm not, and I'm done pretending. It says "Prom Journal" right on it, so my goal is out here in the open. At least in front of Claire.

"I want to go to the prom," I state. "I've spent my entire high school career being the smart girl, and for one night I'm going to be the girl who everyone envies. Including Amber."

"Why?" Claire asks in her wry tone.

"I can't explain it, other than it's like a fingerprint. Proof that I was here. Proof that Chase and I shared something, even if it was unspoken for twelve years. That picture will speak volumes." I shove the journal back into the darkness of my backpack. "Prom produces a photograph and a memory."

"I can make you a picture. I'll get Chase's off his Facebook page. You can pick out your dress online, and I'll cut and paste your head in. Heck, I can even make your boobs bigger." She stares at my chest, which I instinctively cover.

"Forget it. I knew I couldn't come to you about this." I stand up and throw my backpack over my shoulder. "You get a boyfriend and suddenly you've forgotten all about your best friend."

"It has nothing to do with that. You know I couldn't care less about a dance and hanging out with these people. Do I think it's weird your anal-retentive issues have come out in the form of a prom journal? I'm not going to lie to you, Daisy."

"You're not going to help me either."

She blinks innocently. "Meaning?"

"You think Chase is out of my league."

"I don't! I think *you're* out of *his* league."

At that moment, Chase walks in the door and his eyes come straight to mine, but he instantly looks away and seems slightly angry, as though allergic to my gaze. Just by the quickness of his move, I question Gil's advice.

"Let's get out of here," I say to Claire.

"Chase just got here."

"You said yourself if he were interested, I'd know by now."

"I was just ticked off. I didn't mean that. Look, I'm going to be honest. I've never gotten your thing for Chase. He seems all pomp and circumstance without anything real behind him." She stands up. "Come on." She pulls me through the gym, toward the buff jock types that Chase just joined. "If you want him, go get him."

Chase is turned away from us, and I draw in a deep breath as I reach to tap his shoulder, but I'm blinded before I touch him, and the next thing I know, my head is pounding and there's a circle of faces above me.

Chase is standing over me. He doesn't try to help me up. It's as if he believes I'm on the floor by choice. I'm still trying to figure out why I'm on the floor.

"You did that on purpose!" I hear Claire yell. I look up as

130

she wings a basketball toward Britney, Amber's best friend, who's wearing full makeup and stilettos to youth group.

Painfully I realize I've been pounded with a basketball to the face. My fingertips go to my lips, which feel enormous. Chase just stares down at me, like I'm an amusement park attraction.

I maneuver to my feet and bolt toward the door.

"Wait!" Claire yells behind me.

I scramble to my dad's Pontiac and press the alarm button in my haste. Rather than a simple chirp, my dad's aftermarket alarm begins to wail as though the entire town is having a nuclear attack. It goes on and on while I try to break in, pulling frantically at the knob. The doorway fills with teenagers, each more sophisticated than the next in their Abercrombie shirts and designer handbags.

Claire comes alongside me while I press the key remote frantically. She pulls the keys from my hand. "I was wrong," I tell her. "I don't want to be noticed. I want to disappear back into the hole where I came from and never be heard from again." I cover my face. "Photoshop is my friend!" I wail.

Andy, the young minister in charge of youth group, comes out. He's got that cool, Christian rock-star haircut, burly muscles bulging out of T-shirt, and ripped jeans. He's got that hip look and he's so sweet. We're supposed to believe because he's a minister that he would have given us the time of day in high school. But I'm leery.

The alarm blares into the evening sky (which is pink and mocking me), and there's a murmur of giggles from the doorway. I pull at the lever on the car's ancient burgundy door, but nothing happens. Andy slips the keys from Claire, and with a few aimed pushes the wailing dies.

I lean against the car and cover my face again. Claire gives the group an obscene gesture with both hands, and the sight of it makes me fall into laughter. "Stop it," I say.

Only Claire could flip off a church youth group and make it look good and, in her current outfit, preppy. The laughter stops, but the group doesn't dissipate. I wish there was a cop to say, "Nothing to see here. Move along."

Andy hands me back my keys but closes his hand around them at the last minute. "I'm going to have a talk with Britney and her friends. I'm sure they didn't mean to hit you with a basketball."

"Are you really, Andy?" Claire asks. "Or do you just want us to believe that because it's easier than dealing with it?" She shakes her head. "You don't seem to get it. This is our life, Andy. We know they meant it. Daisy has the Angelina Jolie lips to prove it." She looks at me. "It doesn't look as good on you."

"No kidding. Brad Pitt isn't beside me."

"So you're going to let them win?" Andy rests his hand on the roof of the car. "You two seem to think I didn't go to high school. It wasn't that long ago that I had my face shoved in a urinal, or my track shoes heaved over the electrical wire in the street, but you go ahead and leave. Give them more power."

This stops us both, and neither one of us makes a motion to get into the car. Of course, he does still have the keys. "What would you suggest?" I ask.

"Join us for the devotional time. If they make you feel uncomfortable during that, I'll handle it. All right?"

Claire and I look at each other. "It's either that or you slink to school tomorrow while everyone talks behind your back," she says.

I nod and take the keys from Andy. But I do not turn my

dad's cheap alarm system on. "Who does he think is going to steal this piece anyway?"

Claire looks back at the car. "Your father goes through extreme lengths to protect what's his." She makes sure I get her meaning with her squinted eyes.

"I don't want to face Chase," I whisper to Claire. This romance has caused me nothing but pain, and now it's getting physical.

The gym is abuzz when we walk inside. Amber and Britney look over their shoulders with their sly smiles, but no one else seems to notice us, and Andy blows his whistle and calls everyone to order. Chase never even makes eye contact with me. In fact, when I open my mouth, he turns away. He takes the basketball, dribbles it, and shoots a basket. Then he turns to me and grins. Was it a good grin? I have no idea.

The boys start pushing the sofas together, and everyone takes their seats. Britney, long and voluptuous (the voluptuous part rumored to be her sixteenth birthday present), crosses her long, bare legs and stares me down. Meanwhile, my lips are throbbing, and I press them together, wishing I'd never agreed to come back into this room. I'm too optimistic. I keep thinking, *Amber, Britney—they don't mean what they do*, but I'm starting to think differently.

In this room is every reminder that I am not even remotely perfect and I never will be. Hope springs eternal, but so do mean girls.

"Love is patient. Love is kind. Simple, really," Andy says. "Are you patient?" He looks at me. "Are you kind?" He turns his attention to Britney.

"You know, I was wrong," I whisper to Claire. "A night at youth group just may kill you."

❧ 10 ❧

"Daisy, your father and I have fabulous news!" My mother grasps the end of the dining room table, her fingers wrapped around the edges.

"Mom, the last time you used the word *fabulous*, I do believe it involved a shower curtain, which by its very nature cannot be fabulous, as it is plastic and cheesy. Real people have shower doors." I drop my napkin into my lap and focus on the casserole in the middle of the table. "Or by *fabulous*, did you mean on clearance at Walmart?"

"Very funny, Daisy. No, I mean it this time. It's awesome!" she says, which sounds more disturbing than fabulous. Still, she's grinning like a hyena at dusk, and my father has come in ready to share in the kill.

"You'll like this, Daisy. It's a compromise."

"I'm getting a cell phone, but I have to pay the bill?"

"No, nothing like that. Who are you going to call when you're at school and work anyway? I'm always here and you never call me," Mom says.

"Dad, is this news fabulous? Or does it involve either one of you dressing fly and getting jiggy with it in front of my classmates?"

"Jiggy with what?" Dad says. "What are they teaching you at that school? Are you even speaking English?"

My mother hits the table to focus the attention back on her. "Your father and I have been talking about how hard you've worked this year." She winks at my dad from across the table. He pseudo-smiles and plops a huge hunk of the casserole on his plate. Usually my mother serves him—I swear I live in 1957—but he seems to think this may take awhile, so he opts for strenuous work. "Do you want to tell her, honey?"

He raises a palm and shakes his head. Telling me would involve putting his fork down, and that's not going to happen.

"All right, well, I told your father about this dating issue and the prom, and we've decided . . ."

No. No. Please, they can't have decided anything. This is not a simple yes or no, you can go or not. This is something more. There has to be some deep, dark, small print to go along with it. With my parents, there is always the fine print and the soul-of-your-firstborn clause.

"You can go to the dance."

"If someone asks you," my dad adds. "You'll nearly be eighteen by then, and you're right, it will be good practice."

Thanks for the vote of confidence, Dad. "I can?" Read: fine print, please?

"Well, wait a minute. There are some rules."

Did I not say?

"I called the school, and it turns out the prom will be held in a hotel in San Jose. It's the first weekend in March."

"Uh-huh."

"San Jose is a big city, Daisy," Dad says.

"I've heard of it," I say, inwardly rolling my eyes.

"And they'll be needing chaperones."

I look in horror at both of them. I mean, I knew it would be bad, but chaperoning? My mom might as well wear an apron to the dance, or worse yet, her rap getup, and my father . . . there is no question he would wear the tux he wore for his wedding. I know he would. He totally brags about how he got it from the Salvation Army and how Mom has had to let the waist out after all her great cooking, but it still fits. Listen, when your white shirt is popping out of your jacket and your ruffles look victimized, you do not have it, all right?

I look back and forth like it's a tennis match, trying to figure out who would be worse. I swallow the lump in my throat. Mom would be more obvious, but Dad would actually make me dance with him and his bad suit. I opt for Mom.

"And you were thinking?" I manage, shoveling in some casserole so I don't say something I regret.

"Well, your father, of course," my mom says. "He's the one with the tux."

"But," my father says, "they don't let parents chaperone."

"They don't?" I squeal.

"No. Which I don't understand since I pay enough tuition to have some rights at that school."

"Calm down, honey. They don't allow parents, but they do allow pastors from local churches. So we thought if we made a substantial donation to the missions fund—"

"By substantial, you mean more than five dollars? I'm hoping."

"Substantial for us is different from some of the families at church. Pastor understands that."

"Maybe another parent will make a substantial donation and he'll do it."

"If you're going to be a smart aleck, you can just stay home with us, young lady." My dad breathes through his nose, his fork in midair.

"Mom, no offense, but that's hardly letting out the leash, you know? I'm not going to do anything stupid in front of my teachers. They wrote recommendations for me for college. I don't think I need Pastor to hover."

Mom looks hurt. "Well, Daisy, honey, I was only trying to make it happen for you. When your father gave you the purity ring, we thought you understood that this was part of our courtship agreement."

"Mom, I was fourteen, and Hometown Buffet has frozen yogurt with sprinkles on it—that's like waterboarding to a fourteen-year-old. I would have agreed to anything." I see my chance, since my mom is already upset. No use wasting the emotion. It's now or never. "Mom, Dad, I don't want to do a courtship. Sarika, she's totally fine with her dad picking her groom from India, even though she's half English. She trusts her parents because they know who she is, but I'm not sure either of you understands me."

"You're saying you don't trust us?"

"No, I'm saying I don't want to marry a pastor. I have different criteria for marriage than you might have for me. I don't want to end up just waiting on some guy for life. I want a job. A career. I want to go to college for an education, not a man."

"So you want to spend your life alone, is that it?" my father says with his eyebrow cocked.

"At this point, I don't even want to get married. I wanted

to major in finance and have a career in that, but I've been researching neuroscience and—"

"Neuro-what?" My father drops his fork and pushes his plate away. "What is that? One of those majors where you go to school your whole life and never get a job?"

"Dad, we talked about this." Feigning ignorance is his favorite topic. "It's the science of the brain and the central nervous system. How it's organized. It has a few branches, but I think I'm interested in the genetic side of things. I checked, Dad, and I have the perfect prerequisites for it as a major. All my physics and calculus and biology. Claire was right, Dad. I'd be totally bored in finance."

"Claire! You're going to take advice from a girl who works at a hot-dog stand in the mall?"

"You told her that was a good job."

"For her, yes. But—" My dad breaks down and shields his face from me. I stare at my mother. She rises and kneels by my father, putting her arm around him.

"Daisy, can you come back later and eat? I'd like to talk to your father alone."

"Daddy?"

Just go, my mother mouths.

But my dad snuffles, wipes his face with his napkin, and stares daggers at me. "This is because of Claire's father, isn't it? You're hanging around over there with all that money and you think that's the key to life. Going on vacations, fancy cars . . . I told you hanging out with that heathen girl was going to bring nothing but trouble to our Daisy."

"Dad, it's not because of Claire's parents." Seriously? It's because of my parents, but naturally I can't say that. My parents live in abject fear about money. To the point that they have no life whatsoever. Claire's parents honestly think and talk a lot less about money than my own parents. My dad wants to control his own destiny, but he has no idea that if he just got a real job, he'd have a lot more control than what he has now.

"What about Bible college?" my mom asks.

"Mom, I love the idea of Bible college, so I looked it up, and there are Bible colleges that offer certificates in neuroscience." I swallow. "But I'd rather go to UCLA or UC Riverside. Pepperdine if I go with finance."

"Neuroscience," my dad mumbles. "Can't you get something useful, like a teaching degree?"

"Neuroscience is a growing field. I've even researched postgraduate studies at the University of Buenos Aires."

"Buenos Aires!" my father shouts. "So you plan to spend your whole life in school. Just like I said." From the look on my father's face, you would think I've just said I wanted to be a dictator and destroy anything and anyone who stands in my way. "You can major in science at a Bible college."

"I could," I agree. "But"—I suck in a deep breath—"that's not what I want to do."

My mom wails.

"You're welcome to make your own decisions, Daisy. You're nearly a grown woman, but if you choose to go to an unapproved university, I won't pay for it. You've got a dynamic future in front of you, but if you reject God, you'll—"

"I'm not rejecting God."

"You will. At the end of a science degree, you'll come back like all the other know-it-alls and deny that you can't create anything in the laboratory that didn't come from God's design."

"Dad, I'm not turning into Frankenstein. I'm simply fascinated by the human brain and how things work. I have no doubt in my mind that research would only prove God's existence to unbelievers. If you feel more comfortable with me in finance, maybe that's the route I should take."

He shakes his head. "You cannot argue someone into the faith, Daisy. Faith requires . . . well, faith. We don't get to see everything here on earth. There are questions we're simply supposed to have."

This silences me. The line has been drawn. I will turn out like my dad wants or I'm on my own—and ultimately, his failure. I knew what they wanted for me, but I never understood that they wanted it so badly.

"I understand. May I be excused?" I throw my napkin on the table and whisk up my plate. Once in the kitchen, I stare out the rusted, aluminum-framed window. "See what I mean, Lord? My dad has no idea how much energy he loses out of these old windows. Being cheap is costing him. Why does he make those choices?" I wash the dish and set it in the Rubbermaid rack.

The reality hits me as I walk into my bedroom and shut the door. Is it any wonder I want to do things perfectly? A simple conversation about a dance has turned into WWIII about where I'll go to college! My parents' money costs too much, and this existence is like a Band-Aid—I have to rip it away fast. Too slowly and there will be only more pain.

I open my laptop and go to my bank's website. No, I don't have internet in my room, but my neighbors do, and Mrs. Michaels gave me the code to it for watching her cats. So I've had it in my room for over a year. She asks that I try not to slow her husband down around dinner time, but by the time I'm on, they're usually both in bed.

140

I've saved plenty of money from working—and that's with no life. In college, I'll need clothes and travel expenses. I'll need to pay rent. I'll need a job. I'll need prayer and a lot of it.

"It shouldn't be this way, God!" I tell my ceiling. "Why make me choose between college and my parents? I can love you from any school, and Lord, I promise to."

An IM pops up, and instinctively I check the door and click off my bank website. My breath catches. It's Chase.

> DOOG: Daisy, that you?
> DAI$Y: It's me. Hey Chase.
> DOOG: Haven't seen you and you're never online any-more. Wanted to tell you my dad and I are on to tour the Air Force Academy. Got my letter from the senator (TY Amber) and I'm on my way!
> DAI$Y: So cool Chase! When do you go?
> DOOG: First week in March.

My stomach drops. Prom weekend. That's it. There's no one left on my list. Steve Crisco wouldn't ask me anyway. Not unless I gave him the answers for a final, and even then it would be iffy.

> DOOG: Daisy, you there?
> DAI$Y: That's great Chase! So xited 4 u. So u won't be here for the dance.
> DOOG: What dance? Knew u would be. I couldn't wait to tell you. Want to celebrate?
> DAI$Y: Prom. It's the first weekend in March.
> DOOG: Oh, then I'll—

"Daisy?" My mom opens the door and I snap the laptop shut.

"Yeah?" I say in my most innocent voice.

"Honey, your father and I feel like we barely know you lately. Why don't you come out and talk to us? Let's try this again."

"Mom, if I have to major in what you want me to for you to be happy, I don't think there's much to discuss."

She nods. "You're being very selfish, Daisy. Someday you'll understand we want the best for you." She yammers on about Dad's unconditional love for me—the standard guilt-inducing stuff—until she shuts the door again.

I open the laptop. Chase Doogle is offline and so is my life. I exhale. I wish I had the guts to say to him . . . something. Anything that lets him know how he rocks my world. But I have the party to think of and, of course, rearranging Chase's schedule so that he's present for prom. He cannot be my date if he's not here.

Prom Journal
October 1
155 Days until Prom
Fact: One is the loneliest number.

One entry! Let's face it. There was only Chase Doogle. There has always been only Chase Doogle. Everyone else was just my perfectionist persona saying it would be okay if prom wasn't perfect. But that was never true, because I'm a perfectionist. Granted, a perfectionist with a sucky life, but still. A girl has to strive, am I right? But Chase has given me no indication that he'll be here for prom, or that he'd ask me if he were around. Chances are, unrequited love is my destiny.

It's not the photo that matters to me. It never was. I just didn't want to admit how pathetic I am to pine over the same guy for twelve years. He kissed me in kindergarten. Why on earth would I take that as a lifelong commitment?

It's time to focus on Claire's party. Prom is a distant dream if I can't get someone to dance with me in Claire's backyard. Maybe her parents being gone and her living on her own is a gift. Maybe God meant for it to be that way. Yeah. It could happen. And we've decided it's a Christmas party—because nothing says "festive" like a house devoid of parents.

Forty days and forty nights. God may have stopped the rain for Noah, but after forty days, I'm still dry as a bone when it comes to prom prospects. Thanksgiving is approaching, and I do not want to waste the wishbone on something as simple as a prom date. What once seemed so promising now seems hopeless. But for once I am so grateful to have listened to Claire's harebrained idea about the party. It's my only hope if I'm to have a date by Christmas.

Passing glances, casual conversations . . . Chase . . . Max— neither one of them making a move. It's like I'm more repellant than ever.

ȸ ▪ ȿ

"So we've got all the drinks. I borrowed ice chests from the club, so we have to make sure there's enough ice that night. I hired the bouncer. I couldn't find one that looked like Chris Brown. I'd say this guy is more Dwayne 'The Rock' Johnson." Claire maneuvers her Mustang up the curvy, mountainous road that separates the rich people from those of us in the flatlands.

"It's weird how you're so close to my house but totally

separate behind those iron gates. Oh, hey, speaking of which, how are you going to get everyone behind the gate?" She flashes a smile at the guard, and we enter her neighborhood through the owner's open lane.

"I promised the security guard three hundred dollars if he looked the other way." She waves her hand out the window as we leave a trail of kicked-up gravel.

"Three hundred dollars!"

"Don't worry, it's mine. I earned it working at the lemonade stand. Look at my arms." She flexes her muscles, taking her hands off the wheel on the curvy road, so I grab the wheel.

"Hey!"

"Just showing you I earned my own money and I am buff. Max said this would happen, but I didn't believe him."

"When your mom gets home, you are going to be so busted for lying about being alone. The three hundred dollars is going to be the least of your problems."

"Nah, she'll be happy I didn't bug her. I'm showing initiative. She's always telling me to do so. You're the one who needs to worry." Claire is still in her J.Crew phase, which tells the attentive bystander that she's still interested in Greg Connolly, and my prom list is growing infinitely smaller without any help from me. There's so much consistency in her life, I'm honestly starting to worry her parents are a bad influence.

It's hard to imagine that life behind these crisply manicured hills is not absolutely perfect. Though if Claire's house is any indication, that can't be true. At least they've earned the right to control their own destiny and create that facade. I can't help but admire that, even if I know it isn't reality. God does, after all, look at the heart, and I suppose it looks the same behind a beautiful hedge or my shabby, unpainted, periwinkle blue door.

Claire veers off on a side road. "Where are we going?" I ask her.

"I forgot. I have to get one thing at Greg's house. He's going to run the barbecue for me, so he picked up mesquite or something he likes to cook on. I told him I'd put it by the barbecue."

"We're having a barbecue? I thought you said we were ordering pizzas."

"That's for the later guests. The intimate guests arrive at six p.m. Those are the ones we entertain for real. The rest is just for bragging rights."

"My stomach is flipping out. Your father's going to recognize his barbecue has been messed with, and what about your mother's outdoor kitchen?" I cross my arms and sink into the passenger seat. I am getting in deeper and deeper. Granted, further from my perfectionist state, but closer to the criminal mind than I'd hoped for. There has to be a middle ground.

"My mother thinks Marisa is at home looking after me. Do you really think she's going to notice mesquite on the grill? If so, she'll just think Marisa made some fish and didn't want to mess up the kitchen."

I close my eyes. I wish I could talk Claire out of this lame idea, but I know she'll just tell me I sound like my mother and I'm no fun at all. "I shouldn't have ever agreed to this. You took advantage of me when I was high on shopping endorphins. When I had the money to buy jeans. That's just wrong." She pulls the car over to the side of the road. "Wait, Greg Connolly?" My mouth drops. "He's running the barbecue?"

"So?"

"Since when are you and Greg best buddies? Are you two dating?"

"We've been neighbors since kindergarten, Daisy. It's not what you're thinking, get your mind out of the gutter. We're just friends and, you know, neighbors. So he's going to help."

Claire's infamous for making you feel like the guilty party when she's been up to no good. "Has he been over to your house while your parents are gone?" I ask her.

"Daisy, get a life." She steers the car next to the curb. Greg's lawn looks like a football field. The house is set back off the street at the top of a knoll that overlooks the entire city. My heart is in my throat.

"You didn't tell me we were going anywhere! I've got my scruffies on! I thought we were going to work in your back-yard."

"It's your Saturday uniform, what's the big deal? We're just going to be there a second, and Greg won't care. He knows how you dress."

"Are you trying to make me feel better?" I ask.

My heart starts to palpitate. Greg and Chase are on the expansive front lawn, with what looks like a thick, white PVC pipe. I sink into the seat and hide from the window's view, which is no easy task in a Mustang. It's not like my parents' Pontiac, which could house a small family if necessary. "Chase is here." There's no reaction from Claire. "Chase is here," I repeat.

"Well, I didn't know he was going to be here. Just wait here. I'll get the mesquite and be back."

I'm going to kill her. One of these days they're going to find

Claire's body, and I'm going to give police that same innocent look she uses on everyone around her. *What? Who, me?*

"I wouldn't need to confess half my thoughts if it weren't for you, Claire. Hurry up!" I hiss as she exits the Mustang.

I breathe in deeply and silently recite the Lord's Prayer again and again, because otherwise I would have murder on my mind.

Suddenly the passenger door opens and Chase is towering above me. He grins, and I don't even think about the fact that I look like death. His eyes make me forget life around me.

"Claire told me you were in here. I didn't believe her."

"I—I'm in my scruffy clothes. It's Saturday." I get in a fetal position and cover my face.

He nods. "I see that. You look hot in scruffy. More relaxed." He laughs.

"Very funny. Now go away," I say through my hands. I pull at the door handle, but it won't budge.

"Come see the rocket we made. It's for Physics. Anytime you can use explosives and call it a homework project, Greg and I are all over it. He's going to be a munitions expert, you watch." He puts his hand on mine and I forget to breathe. "Come on, we're going to test it. It's going to be momentous, like the flight of the Kitty Hawk."

"This isn't going to end up on *America's Funniest Videos*, is it?"

"Hope not. We'd get an F if that happened." He tugs and pulls me out of the seat. I hike my baggy jeans higher onto my waist.

The sun is blinding, and the lush green grass is like something from an English estate, with the exception of the propulsion equipment at the center of it. I shield my eyes and read the address. "3618," I say. "This is where Greg lives?"

Chase nods. It feels like everyone else in the world has the secret to being rich, but it's escaped my family.

"That's the number of miles Captain Bligh traveled after the mutiny on the *Bounty*. He sailed it in a twenty-three-foot dinghy with only a compass and the stars. Saved his men."

Chase stares at me.

I shrug. "You want to be an Air Force hero, Bligh was a naval hero," I explain, wishing I could take back my stupid factoid. "I remember facts."

"I've noticed. It's cute."

Chase keeps my hand in his as we walk over to the PVC pipe rocket he and Greg have made. "We have enough rocket fuel in here." He puts his hand on his hip. "At night? This thing is going to light up like Halley's Comet. But we want to practice during the day first so we don't have to take into account the wind. The morning is calmest."

"They were thinking about making some for the party," Claire says as we approach her and Greg.

"Just what we need for the party, explosives. What about the zero tolerance policy at school?" I ask Greg, sounding remarkably like my mother.

Claire hears my question and scowls at me. She's right.

Greg heaves the rocket launcher onto his shoulder. "We've got three stages on the rocket. Should hit close to a mile." He puts it down and seals the cap on the back.

"Greg, I'm no rocket expert, but I don't think you have a mile up here."

Claire scowls again.

"Don't you have to go to work?" I ask her.

"Three stages." Greg grins. "D engines, each with their own ignition. Light her up, let's see what she can do."

I have a sick feeling in my stomach. Not because I don't trust Chase and Greg, but because I'm grounded for missing homework again, and I'm at a guy's house in my worst possible outfit—and trust me, that means something for me. And somehow I know . . .

The rocket launcher is ignited, and a small sizzling sound is followed by a blast with such a kickback that Greg ends up on the grass. He never takes his eye off the rocket, which whistles through the air. Chase is videotaping the rocket. "Woo-hoo, the second stage is lit!" The rocket climbs higher.

But at the third stage, something clearly goes wrong. The rocket takes a turn for the ground and launches to the dry grasses that surround the manicured lawn. In an instant, a small ball of fire erupts and sets the field on fire.

We all stare at each other. Chase runs with the hose to the end of the grass, but he gets nowhere near the fire when the hose runs out of mileage. "Call 9-1-1!" he shouts.

Naturally, no one has their phone on them, so Greg runs toward the fire and yells for us to run into the house. My legs are sweating as I hightail it to the massive front doors decorated with black wrought iron over the windows. I burst through the double French doors and find a couple staring at me, a king-sized bed behind them. Apparently I've stepped into the master bedroom rather than the front door. I'm too panicked to bother explaining a thing.

"Call 9-1-1, the field's on fire!" Meanwhile I'm thinking, *Who has double doors and a master bedroom at the front of their house?*

Mrs. Connolly, an elegant redhead in capris and a collared

shirt, drops a bottle of perfume and grabs the phone. "I told you to watch him!" she shouts at her husband. "I am going to kill that kid! If you weren't so self-absorbed in your baseball games, you might have noticed your son is a pyromaniac!"

"So now he's my son, is he? I didn't raise him alone, you know! Maybe if you'd treated Greg as one of your charity events, he might have gotten enough attention!" Mr. Connolly rushes outside through the open doors to assess the situation, comes back in, disappears deeper into the house, and returns with a red fire extinguisher, all within seconds. It's as if I'm standing still while time is in fast-forward.

Mrs. Connolly is on the phone with the operator when she looks out the window and tells her, "I think my son and husband may have stopped it from spreading, but hurry. Hurry!" She slams down the phone and starts speaking with her hands. "Harvard wants this kid. He has set this house on fire twice, taken apart absolutely everything electronic we own, and Harvard wants him. At this point, I'm glad someone does!" She finally notices my presence. "Who are you?"

"I'm Daisy."

"Daisy Crispin?"

I nod.

"Well, little Daisy Crispin, I haven't seen you since Greg's fifth grade swim party. Didn't you grow up to be a beauty? Forgive my outburst. I don't know what came over me."

"Well, your lawn's on fire. It's understandable."

"How did this happen?" she asks rhetorically.

I don't know. Why do you let your son play with explosives in the front yard? Do you have an explanation for that?

"I . . . Claire—" This is where Claire usually comes in with one of her excuses. On my own, I'm stupefied. Two white

151

fire engines appear at the curb, and I use the chaos to make my escape out of the house.

Greg's father has turned the automatic sprinklers on, so there's no chance of the fire jumping the line to the house, but the flames have petered out down the hill anyway and much of the excitement is over. Only the strong smell of smoke and a few sparks remain. Greg stands near his father and films the billows of smoke on his video camera.

"I guess you're not going to work today," I say to Claire. Her car is blocked by the fire trucks.

"When I get scared, Greg comes and stays, but it's not what you're thinking. His room is at the other end of the house. His parents never know he leaves." She looks over at the horizon, watching the firemen.

I follow her. "That was not a sufficient answer."

"No, Mrs. Crispin, it wasn't meant to be." She stalks off toward Greg.

"Sorry about the show," Chase says as he walks over. "Maybe you were right about *America's Funniest Videos*. We should have taped it. I threw the recorder down when the field caught." If Chase were a dog, his tail would be between his legs. "I knew I shouldn't have let Greg shoot it. He's such a hot dog."

"Hey," Greg yells. "I was smart enough to pick up the camera, wasn't I? Without it, we wouldn't have a project. We'll be heroes now!"

"Heroes? For setting your chemistry project on fire?"

"Shut up, I'll have to edit you out!" Greg says and stalks closer to the fire and out of earshot.

"Chase?"

"Yeah, Daisy?"

"Greg wouldn't do anything stupid, would he?" Which feels like the most inane question, considering the idiocy I'm watching unfold. "I mean, he wouldn't take advantage of someone in trouble? Like a girl?"

"Greg? Nah, he wouldn't hurt a fly."

I stare at Greg while his father reads him the riot act at the edge of the grass, but what I notice is that Greg's hand is currently intimately acquainted with Claire's backside. *I should have told my parents! What if Claire's in trouble and my own silence caused it?*

I shake my head.

"What?" Chase asks.

"I have to call Claire's mom."

"What? Why? Everyone is counting on your party. It's been the talk of the school. If Claire's mom comes home . . ." He lets his voice trail off.

My mind goes in a million directions. If Claire's mom comes home and we cancel this party, we are dirt at St. James and I am dirt with Claire, but she's always been the strong one. The girl able to resist peer pressure and dress the way she wanted, act the way she wanted. She treated guys like lost puppies lucky to be in her shadow. Seeing Greg's hand on her backside, ever so briefly . . . It's like something changed.

"She's not the same person." I shake my head. "There's not going to be a party. Claire needs her parents right now, even if she doesn't think so."

Chase steps toward me and wrinkles his nose. It's my favorite expression of his. He looks so manly and yet so adorable at the same time. "Daisy, the whole school is counting on this. You can wait until Christmas break to call her parents. Claire's already been alone for so long. What's going to change now?"

"What if one day does make a difference? You want me to wait over a month?"

"Just until the party's over. A couple weeks, that's all."

I nod toward Greg. "Has he grown up to be a decent guy?"

"Who, Greg? Heck yeah. Daisy, what are you so worried about? We're not children anymore. What do you think is going to happen? It's a party. They happen every week."

"Not for us," I say, humiliated by my own admission. "I don't know. Maybe living in the present wasn't such a good idea after all. Maybe we were better off invisible."

Chase stares at me with that look I've always garnered from kids like him. The one that makes me feel like I need a straitjacket.

A policeman approaches with what's left of the three-stage rocket in his bulging hands. The rocket had a parachute attached, which is now nothing more than a web of ashes dangling on some severed strings. "This belong to you?"

Chase reaches out, but the officer drops the rocket to his side on the grass.

"Not so fast. We have some questions for you and your friends."

"There are no explosives, Officer. It's a project for Physics. Everything is slow burn, stable, just a sugar mixture, and we got carried away with the stages. We didn't think it would fly that far, but it's perfectly street legal."

"Not when it's aimed at dry grass in a residential neigh-borhood."

"It wasn't aimed!" I shout. "I just lost control of it. It got away from me." I try to remember my physics, but I'm so nervous. My hands are shaking. All I know is if Chase Doogle gets taken in, his days at the Air Force Academy are over, and by comparison, I have nothing to lose.

"Let me see your hands." I hold them out. Chase does too. The officer walks away to question Claire and Greg.

Chase takes my outstretched hands, which are shaking. He's not shy today. Maybe my lack of makeup, a hairbrush, and real pants helped that scenario.

"Just go home, Daisy. I'll be fine. What we did is perfectly legal." He steps toward me, and his eyes stare right through me. I could melt under them. I hear my heart beating as he gets closer, and I close my eyes to remember this moment and all its perfection. It's like making that curlicue of chocolate perfection right on top of a truffle.

"There's nothing sexier than a girl willing to fight for me. Little Daisy Crispin, my first love. My Daisy Crispin." His smile develops slowly, and then his finger's at my nose. "But let's get one thing straight. I fight for my girl. She doesn't fight for me."

He pecks my cheek with a chaste kiss. My first grown-up kiss, even if it was like something my grandfather would grace me with. Somehow I always knew I'd hear sirens and see fireworks. I just didn't know they'd be real.

"So when you say 'my Daisy Crispin'—"

"Daisy Crispin!" I hear my father's voice and stiffen.

"Did you say something?" I ask Chase, but his eyes are wide, and he shakes his head to tell me to shut up. Slowly I turn around.

My father, dressed like a pirate sporting his sagging, stuffed parrot, marches toward me. The Pontiac is blocking the cop car. A journalist snaps his picture as he approaches, and I try to think fast. Why am I standing on a boy's front lawn in my scruffies, being questioned by the police and eerily close to Chase Doogle? Of course, my father has to show up dressed like he works at Long John Silver's, and I half expect him to break into song. This is my life! Girls like me do not get to go to prom. Girls like me end up as statistics in the back of the yearbook: *Additional photography by Daisy Crispin.*

"You want to introduce us, Daisy?"

Not really. Could you take the parrot off first? "Dad," I say through clenched teeth. "What are you doing here?" He knows good and well who Chase is, and this sudden amnesia is meant to humiliate me into quiet submission.

"I wanted to know what you and Claire were up to. Your mother has been trying to call Claire's mother and hasn't been able to reach her. It appears she's changed her cell number. I thought I'd make a trip to Claire's house to ask her parents about their beliefs on courtship, make sure they were honoring our wishes for our daughter."

My heart is pounding. Had he gone to Claire's house, he would have found out her parents are not in town. Nor have they been. Nor will they be. And as bad as it is that I'm standing on a guy's front lawn practically in his arms, I think the alternative might be worse.

"Dad, you remember Chase Doogle from kindergarten? Chase, this is my dad." I smile maniacally. "Dad, Chase is going to the Air Force Academy. He wants to fly, and this was part of his Physics project. Claire and I were passing by on our way to her house—"

My dad rips the parrot off his shoulder. "Be quiet for a minute, Daisy."

"Dad, Chase was testing a theory on jet propulsion and—"

"Get in the car."

"Dad." I try to get his attention off Chase, but he won't even look at me. It's like I'm a rodeo clown and my dad is the bull who has eyes only for the guy he bucked.

"I'm sure you're a very nice kid, but stay away from my daughter. She's got a future in front of her, and she's not going to screw it up over a guy, got it? We are a family that believes in courtships, and since Daisy has no intention of marrying in the near future, we see no reason for her to be in fellowship with boys her age."

"Yes, sir."

I'm gonna die. I'm gonna die. Right here and now, on Greg Connolly's front lawn. Just dig me a hole, throw me in, and place a cross over me. I'm done.

"Daisy, get in the car."

I do so because if he sees the ice chests or finds out what Claire and I were up to this time, Chase Doogle's presence is going to be the least of my problems. I feel four inches tall, and I can't even look at Chase until I'm safely behind the car's window. I don't want to know what he thinks. It's as if my heart is being ripped from my chest. My dream was so close. I held it in my hand, and just like that rocket, it soared to new heights only to come crashing back to earth in a blaze of glory.

The police are still taking Greg's statement, and I watch as Chase walks toward the officer, then turns back toward me.

"Chase," I say to the window. He doesn't take his eyes off me as my dad starts the car and pulls away from the curb. Chase gets smaller and smaller until we turn a curve and he disappears altogether.

I hear myself let out a sob. "How could you, Daddy?" When I get home, I'm going to look up the cheapest, furthest college from Silicon Valley, and if I have my way, I am never, ever coming back. "I can enlist!" I shout. "I'm used to rules and fighting for everything. I can enlist."

"What did you say?" my father asks. "No, forget it. Don't say anything to me. Right now I am so mad at you. Your mother needed help this morning, and where are you? Off on some guy's lawn. You and Claire just take off like you answer to no one, and that is not how I run my household."

"I can enlist in the armed forces. Oh my gosh, I bet it will even feel like freedom after my childhood!"

"You are not enrolling in the armed forces. Daisy, you can't even make it through a war movie."

"I can too."

He looks at me. "Which one?" He starts to whistle. He whistles when the tension rises, to block any opposition or actual conversation. A nasty habit he has in the car, as if we aren't obvious enough in our old clunker. Please, open your window and whistle so the world doesn't miss us on parade.

"*The Sound of Music*," I say, crossing my arms. "There were Nazis in it and everything!"

"I'll tell you what, you make it through *Band of Brothers* or *Apocalypse Now*, and I'll drive you to the recruiting station. What happened to UCLA? Venezuela?"

"Argentina," I correct him. "It's not my fault. You won't let me see an R-rated movie, or I would have watched more."

"So it's my fault you're not cut out for the military."

"I guess it is. I'm glad you're big enough to admit it."

"I'll make a deal with you."

158

My dad's deals are slightly fairer than the Taliban's. "I'm listening."

"You quit your job, go to Bible college where I know you'll be safe, and you can be trusted to have more of a social life. Then, when you're old enough, you can finish at whatever school you'd like."

"Quit my job! I can't quit my job." It's my only sanity. "I know I've had a lot of long hours, but that's over after one more week. I want a car when I'm at college, and no offense, but I'm not taking this one. If I don't have a car, I won't be able to get around."

"I'm not offering you this car. All teenagers think their parents know nothing, but then they grow up and realize maybe their parents weren't quite as ignorant as they thought."

"Yeah, somehow I see it differently, and it's not because I'm a teenager. Dad, look at this neighborhood!" We're driving through a winding road where each mansion is bigger and more magnificent than the next. "You can't tell me every person here should live just like us. It's not realistic, Dad. People are different. Remember when we watched that *House Hunters* in the Czech Republic and every house was exactly the same because it was all built by communism? Is that what you want for me? To have the same and not strive for greatness? Is that what you think God wants from me? Mediocrity?"

"You have no idea the dysfunction that goes on behind beautiful doors. All that beauty does is mask what really happens."

I could admit right now that Claire's parents are splitting, but I don't. "They have no idea the dysfunction that goes on behind our desperately-in-need-of-paint door! Nobody's perfect, Dad. I don't understand why you think Bible college is going to be safe. I could get run over by a garbage truck. I could get locked in a refrigerator as a harmless prank—"

"You could marry a fine preacher and have 2.7 children and a perfectly contented life."

"I could, Dad. You just can't make it happen. That's all I'm saying."

His cheek flinches.

"If I became a neuroscientist and found the cure to restoring brain function, would you see that as a failure?"

"God won't measure you on your financial success or your career. You've put so much work into that job of yours, and for what? A rich kid who won't appreciate a lick of it? You miss dinner every night for him?"

"Gil is a good boss, Dad. He's really fair with me financially, and he wrote an excellent reference for my college applications."

"He wrote it, or you wrote it for him?"

"What's the difference?"

"Ahh!"

"Daddy." I soften my voice. "What if we focused on prom in March and forgot about weddings and my career? What if we let me be seventeen?"

"What if we focus on getting you to adulthood? I'm hardly worried about your social life at this point. You obviously have plenty of friends."

"Yeah, no doubt." Is he kidding me? I have been thirty-five since I was twelve. If anyone needs to grow up, it's the guy in the pirate suit beside me.

Prom Journal
112 Days until Prom

Fact: He said my name. Destiny's Child would be proud.

He called me "my Daisy." He might even have been willing to change the date of his travel. If my father didn't have the worst timing alive, I'd know. I would have asked.

He could have meant "my Daisy" with a gentle pat to the head, but he could also have meant it with a fire in his eyes that Christian girls aren't supposed to dream about. But realizing that he makes my heart pound puts so much more tension into the situation. That was the point of my prom journal. Not to be a perfectionist. To get one date who would look good in the picture. That's what this was about. Not obsessing over a guy I've loved since kindergarten.

I have one entry on my prom list and 112 days left to bag him. God forgive me, I know "bag him" is not the best choice of words, but I'm getting desperate here!

1. ~~Brian Logan.~~ Wandering hands that are wandering nowhere near me, regardless.

2. Steve Crisco. My only alternative option, so I really have to step up the tutoring to twice a week if I want him to be presentable. Lord have mercy if he goes telling my parents his surfing-for-Jesus scheme. I will be in an all-girls' college faster than you can say "solitary confinement," and they still haven't agreed to prom yet!

3. ~~Greg Connolly.~~ Clearly has a thing for my BFF.

Cannot break girl code for a date. It would taint the photo. Plus he's a bit too pyro for me.

4. ~~Kelvin Matthews.~~ Escaped my grasp to another school when his father got laid off. I wonder if he suspected?? Was a weight lifted from him?

5. ~~Chase Doogle.~~ Sigh. I will never learn. Even with two lines through his name, I still want to scribble "Daisy Doogle." But I can't do that. If I have any expectations with Chase, my heart will only get broken. I can't afford that.

❧ 12 ❧

Checks R Us has ramped up production. With the banking crisis, the factory is churning twenty-four hours a day to keep up with all the checks being printed with new bank names. Which would be a great thing if they didn't keep up with an equal number of mistakes as well.

Between my duties on the phone and taking over accounts payable, life has become one giant spreadsheet. It keeps me from obsessing about my prom date (or lack thereof), Claire's party (okay, mine too, if I'm honest)—which grows bigger by the minute—and if I'll have enough to make ends meet for college.

That's not completely true. Every night I look at the phone and imagine the conversation with Chase—where I tell him how I feel and he whispers sweet nothings in my ear.

On an up note, Gil bought me a company BlackBerry with unlimited texting. My work has paid off, though he didn't let me get pink. He said when I was off to college, my replacement might be a guy. Whatever. Now if only I had someone to text, life would be even better. Claire officially has become an event planner. Sarika can't text and Angie just wants to talk about math. Who knew my friends were so boring?

I power down the computer for the night. "I'm a loser," I say to Lindy.

"Good, then you can close up. See you tomorrow." She bolts for the door and doesn't give me time to answer.

Gil steps out of his office and startles me.

"Gil, I didn't know you were in here! I thought you were in the factory." He has that bed-head look that he spends lots of time and product on, so I assume he was in his office primping for this woman who keeps calling.

"So you're talking to yourself, is that what you're saying?"

"I'm my own best company, you know."

"Want a ride home? I'm going to get out of here early tonight. Now that I've given you the phone, you can call for help, so I figure it's a safe offer."

"Until we get to my dad." I laugh. "I hope you're heading to your girlfriend's house because she's driving Lindy crazy."

"She's not my girlfriend. She's sort of *Fatal Attraction* meets *Bridget Jones*, and I can't lose her. Got any ideas?"

"Nope, losing potential mates just comes natural to me." I zip my backpack and toss it over my shoulder. "I'll see you tomorrow."

He stares at me and shakes his head. "Daisy, stop ignoring me. I asked if you wanted a ride home."

"I'll take the bus."

"It's dark out. I don't want you taking the bus. Where's your father?"

"He doesn't like coming out at night once he's settled in."

"Daisy, how long have you worked here?"

"Fourteen months and three days." I shrug. "It's a math thing, don't mind me."

"Is it that you don't trust me?" he asks.

"Not at all!" I force shock into my voice. "It's that my parents are really particular about where I am and who I'm with, and I don't want to answer their questions. You know, about the phone and my time here." I laugh. "They seem to assume the worst of me."

"We have that in common." Gil slides through life with ease, and his effortless polish is unnerving. Gil would never entertain ideas of me, but it dawns on me that I'd be out of my league if he did. My breath quickens as I think of myself as that poor, desperate woman calling here all day. She's not the first, and judging by Gil's guiltless, handsome grin, she won't be the last. "Call your father and tell him I'm bringing you home. That way he has the option of coming to get you. It's not safe for you to ride that bus alone at night." Gil frowns. "I'll never understand your father. Instead of that useless purity ring, he should have bought you cab fare."

I follow him out the door without calling my dad, and he locks up behind us. "Could you give me a ride to the bus stop? I'll be fine from there. The bus lets out right in front of my house." I'm wishing I'd just called Claire. There's nothing worse than telling other people how controlled my life really is—at least Claire knows.

"I'll drive you to the end of your street, all right? I'd feel better about that." His smile is warm, and I'm humiliated by my previous darker thoughts.

"Yeah, that'd be great. I have a lot of homework, so the earlier I get home, the better."

"Are you ever going to buy yourself a car? You're earning a lot for a girl your age."

"I'm saving my money for college. My dad doesn't want

to pay for where I want to go. By the time I paid insurance and the car payment, it wouldn't be worth it."

"I suppose if I lived like you, with more self-restraint, I'd be working for someone other than my father. You're a smart girl, Daisy. By the way, you never said what your dad thought about the BlackBerry. Was he impressed you earned a company phone?" He rattles his keys. "You didn't tell him, did you?"

I shrug.

"Still keeping secrets, are you? Daisy, I know I've told you how important it is to state your dreams and goals, or your father will be like mine and make those goals for you." He looks back at the office. "I could have stayed in Boston. Could have gone to New York. Instead, I'm here with all the engineers and the women who love them."

I laugh. "It's not that bad. You don't have to be lonely, Gil. You choose it." Besides, if I could tell Gil the truth, that I'd kept Claire's parents' absence a secret all this time, that I'd kept my parents away from the mission of calling hers, he'd be proud. But I can't tell him, of course. Because the party is a secret. Unless you are someone at St. James Academy and you've been invited by my illustrious best friend or me.

"You wait until you're twenty-one and want to have a night life. You'll see. Mark my words, if you don't take control of your life now, you're handing it over to your dad forever."

"It's not like you have to stay. Tell your father you're going. Go get a job somewhere else."

He nods under the streetlight and fingers a piece of hair down into place. "Tell me that in seven years. Tell me how easy it is then. You seem to think I don't know what it's like to have an overinvolved parent, but you're seeing your future here. I'm stopped by some unseen force that probably isn't even there, but it might as well be." He bends over me and opens the door to his Porsche.

"If my future includes a Porsche, I'm not sure I have anything to worry about. I've never been in a sports car before. Well, besides Claire's Mustang." Crawling into the sports car is a lesson in gymnastics. One has to wonder if there's a graceful way to enter a Porsche. If there is, I haven't learned it.

"You become as valuable to your next boss and maybe that will be your next perk. I'll be happy to give you a reference when you're off for school. Though I'd rather you just stay here and do junior college." He turns the key in the ignition, and the engine roars to life. "It never occurred to me to hire a high school student, but my dad knew what he was doing when he hired you. I guess once in a while the old man does know what he's doing."

"Your father came to the high school to speak about his businesses. I'm fascinated by him. He's got so many irons in the finance fire that I couldn't stop wondering, how does a person get like that? Where they can manage so many different things at once and keep all the balls up in the air. I knew this was the place for me if he'd hire me, so I simply asked."

Gil laughs. "Here I thought my dad had found a needle in a haystack. You're telling me you found him? It's just like him to take credit for you."

"Well, I wouldn't say he did that."

Gil steps on the gas, and my neck is tugged by the velocity. He weaves in and out of traffic like a video game, and all I can think of is the coroner explaining to my father how I ended up in a twenty-four-year-old's Porsche with a mystery cell phone. *She was such a responsible child too.* "One stupid action," my dad would say in his sermon voice. "One stupid move is all it took, and she's gone. Gone." In my imagination, my dad shows no remorse over my untimely demise, only disappointment that it's my own fault.

"C-could you slow down, Gil?"

He comes to a hard stop at the light. "My dad didn't buy you a BlackBerry, though, did he?"

"Nope. That was definitely your idea."

The tires peel as he takes off at the green light. I'm short of breath. I decide it's best to get the conversation away from Gil's dad and any leftover childhood animosity brewing in his adrenaline-charged head.

"My parents don't think much of technology. That's why I didn't tell them about the phone. I only got a laptop because my physics teacher told my dad I'd need one for college. My dad loves the idea of physics for me, until it involves an actual major."

"Physics, huh?"

"My second love. After finance. I love that it's so easy. You simply spend less than you take in, and everything works out in a nice, neat equation. Sometimes with a remainder. If you understand the rule of seventy."

"You are such a nerd. Are you serious?"

"Thanks, Gil. I needed that reminder."

"I'm just kidding. I didn't know anyone like you in high school."

"We were there, Gil. You just didn't notice us. It's the story of my life. Popular kids stay on one side of the school and nerds on the other. You probably weren't even aware there was an entire population of us at your school. We'd still be invisible if Claire's video hadn't gone viral."

"Is there a particular guy you want to notice you? What type of guy is he? Brainiac like you, or the jock type?"

"I don't know. Both. I guess."

"Oh, you want it all. I should have recognized that about you. You're not one to settle."

"It's not like that."

Working in a small office has its perks—it's easy to get noticed if you work hard—but on the annoying side, there are no boundaries in a small office. Everyone knows your business and thinks they have a right to all the answers. It's just an extension of my home life. It seems everyone wants to comment on why I'm such a wreck.

"Look, it's no one special, Gil. I'm focused on my grades, getting into the right college. I just need a prom date so high school isn't a total loss. But this week is our party, so I'm planning on an all-out assault."

"A prom date?" He laughs at me. "Go with a group of friends. You'll have more fun and the guy won't be trying to—" He clears his throat. "Prom is overrated. I'm glad you're not looking seriously at anyone. You have plenty of time for that. Look at me. I'm twenty-four and I'm just now starting to look around and see what's out there. What life has to offer. There's no hurry to grow up."

"Stop that."

"What?"

"Telling me what I want. Why does everyone think they know what I want? I'm not a child."

"I never said you were! You sound like a woman to me right now. Screaming at me."

"Women wouldn't scream at you if you called them back. Showed them some respect."

169

"That's what you want? A guy who respects you? All girls say that."

"Maybe because it's true."

He snickers. "Do you want to be respected or get a date? I'll tell you how to get a date."

"A date with a guy like you? No thanks."

"I'm hurt." Gil looks over at me, his face lit by the street-light, his eyes on my bare legs. I yank at my skirt. Gil is persuasively charming, which is why I've generally kept my distance from him. He may not be interested in me in that way, but Gil has a way of making every woman feel as though she's the only one. I look at him, and he abruptly removes his eyes from my legs and presses the gas pedal with vigor.

"You're not half bad," he says.

"Thanks, I think."

"Most girls do something with themselves, that's all I'm saying. You don't even try. You give off that vibe that you don't care, so we guys don't think you do."

"I don't have any vibe!"

"You do. It's like you're too good for us. Too smart for us. Girls like you are so serious. I mean, don't get me wrong. When guys want to get married, you're totally the girl they're going to call, but if you want a boyfriend . . . Well, in high school, guys want a girl that other guys want."

I sit back in the seat and cross my arms. "You cannot tell me all guys are as small-minded as that."

"True, I can't, but I can tell you a good majority of them are."

"Chase doesn't think like that."

"Chase?"

"Just a guy I've gone to school with my whole life. He's going into the Air Force Academy."

"Well, if Chase doesn't think like that, why isn't he your boyfriend?"

"It's complicated."

"Don't tell me your parents have rules about that too."

I wish that were the only reason. "We're just friends, Chase and me."

"Ah!" He punches a fist to his chest. "The worst rejection of them all. Did he say that?"

"He hasn't said anything. I barely see him."

Gil pulls the car over to the side of the road and stares at me. He is blissfully handsome, and for a moment I wish I were slightly older, slightly more worldly. He slides open his ashtray and pulls out a business card. "This is my sister. She owns her own hair salon."

I hold the card. "That's great. She's got her own business?"

"She's got her own business because she knew what she wanted, and she didn't let my father tell her styling hair was a ridiculous profession. Now, her shop is the talk of the town in Los Gatos. She charges two hundred dollars for a haircut, and she teaches in hair shows across the country. She's really living her dream."

"Two hundred dollars!" I exclaim and let go of the card.

He writes something on the back of it. "You take this to her. Chelsea is her name. You tell her I sent you and I'll pay for anything you want done."

"Why?"

"Because guys your age want the girl everyone wants."

"A hairstyle isn't going to make me that, Gil." I laugh.

"What if I don't look like that girl when all is said and done? And barring major surgery, I don't see how it would."

"The haircut is nothing. It's the level of confidence you project that makes guys take notice. You treat the guys as badly as you treat your boss, and you're home free."

I hesitate to take the card.

"Daisy, I'm not doing these things because I want anything from you. I'm doing them because I want you to make different choices than I did, to find out what you want in this life and take it before someone does it for you."

As I take the card and place it in my backpack, my confidence level grows by leaps and bounds. "A haircut. A real one, not one my mom does at the living room table, but one with professional shampoo and a blow-dry?" I cover my mouth. I think I just squealed in front of Gil. "Thank you, Gil."

"Thank *you*, Daisy. I know you do a lot more for the business than I can afford to pay you. I wish just one of the full-time girls had your computer skills." He smiles in a fatherly way, and for some reason I am beaming with pride.

"No one would ever consider you a failure, Gil. I sure wish you'd stop considering yourself that. You've taken that company to a different level, and it's only getting better."

He merges back into traffic and I see him grin. Life is full of surprises. Not the least of which is my boss.

My first act of treason is going to be this week's party. My second? Dyeing my hair without my mom's permission. As far as acts of rebellion go, coloring my hair (a normal color, meaning one in the realm of believability) is probably considered lightweight on the scale of defiance.

13

Friday, December 3
Mood: Nervous
Fact: There are over two million sweat glands in the human body. I am using all of them.

Tonight is the night. I have bathed myself in prayer and I'm going to take Gil's advice. I'm going to make my feelings known to Chase and suffer (or reap) the consequences. I need to know if, by "my Daisy," he meant it in the come-hither, I-want-you way, or the this-is-my-little-sister way.

"It's better to know, right?" I say to Claire as she lights luminaries on the brick path.

"Less talky, more worky."

"Why are we using luminaries? Can't you turn on the lights? Luminaries seem so Martha Stewart. Martha is not cool."

"Because it's so *Gossip Girl*. It goes with the theme."

"We have a theme?"

"Remember, I taped all the *Gossip Girl* episodes, so I'm going to show them on the big screen outside. That way, if couples want to relax, they can stretch out on the grass and watch Blair Waldorf start some real trouble."

"I'm not even allowed to watch that show," I remind her. "Where do you put luminaries in Manhattan?"

"Shut up. You're not allowed to be at my house without my parents here, you're not allowed to be at Greg's house in your scruffies, and you're not supposed to have a BlackBerry, and yet here you are worrying about my choice of light source. Makes you wonder, huh?"

"Claire." I pace the pathway. "I don't have a good feeling. Maybe we should just call the whole thing off."

"It sort of helps if you start your sentences a few words back, so I have some kind of clue what you're talking about. We're not calling the party off. If you've gone prophetess on me suddenly, God probably has a better use for it than spouting doom about our party."

"I'm not prophesying. I just have a bad feeling."

"That's from all the lying. You'll get over it. Go get dressed, the guys will be here in half an hour." She lights the last luminary. "I'll be upstairs in my room." She slams her front door.

I sink down on the steps. This would be so much easier without guilt. Without conscience. "I feel sick to my stomach."

A black Mercedes pulls up into the driveway, and Max steps out of the car and looks at me over its rooftop. "Hi, Daisy."

"Hi, Max. How'd you get in here? We didn't pay off the security guard until nine."

"I told him in broken English that I was the gardener. Last-minute stuff before the party."

"A gardener who travels in a Mercedes?"

"What can I say? I'm a good gardener."

"We hired a bouncer," I tell him. "So you don't need to protect us from anything."

"Claire fired the bouncer. He came to stake out the place, and he scared her."

"She did not."

"Ask her," Max says.

"What are you really doing here?" I cross my arms. "You're fashionably early, which is impossible. Early is just rude."

"I'm here to watch out for you."

"Watch out for me?" I laugh. "I'm going to a party. What's the worst thing that could happen? I'd have too much fun?"

He shuts his car door and comes to sit next to me on the steps. He smells divine. "Wow, this is some view up here."

"It's amazing, isn't it?" I'm caught staring at him when he turns. "You have the most amazing bone structure." I feel his jaw. "It's like you're always sucking in your cheeks, but it's totally natural, huh?"

He starts to laugh. "Cut it out, that tickles. So what am I to believe? That I have dimples and a birth defect? Or amazing bone structure?"

"Well, both, of course." I put my hands back in my lap.

"At home, they say I look like Ivan without the blue eyes."

"Who?"

"He's a famous model. His dimple—excuse me, birth defect—is in his chin. He starred as Nacho on the soap opera *Calientes*."

"You have a soap opera called *Hot*? Is Paris Hilton in it?" I start to giggle uncontrollably. Usually this is where I'd insert some inane fact, but this time I'm not even tempted.

"Daisy, let's blow this Popsicle stand. Let me take you out. Come with me, and let me show you how to tango. We'll have asada." He smirks. "Steak."

"Steak?" My eyes brighten. I look behind me and giggle nervously. "I would love to see you explain that one to my father."

"We'll stop there on the way."

"You're sweet, Max. I'd like nothing more, to tell you the truth, but I can't leave Claire. She's not in a good place tonight, and I'm sort of the designated parental unit. I'm worried about the house. She acts like she's fine, but I worry if someone starts to destroy something, she'd just let them."

He breathes in deeply. Every move he makes is utterly fascinating and effortless.

"You remind me of my boss in some ways."

"Why, is he devastatingly handsome?"

"Actually, yes."

"Oh. So when are you quitting this job? I can't take the competition."

"I wouldn't call him competition. He calls me 'jail bait.'"

"An older man. More opposition. I do not like this," he says in a thick Spanish accent.

"You use that accent at will, don't you?"

He raises his brow. "When it suits me, maybe."

"I'm not worthy, so save yourself the effort." I stand up and pat him on the knee. "The guests are going to be here any minute. I have to get dressed. Thanks for the offer, Max."

"The dreaded knee pat." He throws the back of his hand to his forehead. But then he stands up and turns somber. "I can't let you stay here, Daisy. If you do, I'm going to have to call the police."

176

I laugh. "The police? It's not illegal to have a party, Max. We're not serving any alcohol. I promise."

"Roofies are illegal."

"What's that? Some kind of candy?"

"Roofies are a fact you don't know, huh?" he says. "Interesting."

"Max, you're scaring me. Why are you so serious? What are you talking about?"

He takes my hands in his, which have perfect structure as well. "Everyone at school thinks I'm Mexican, right?"

"I guess."

"Rohypnol. It's a date-rape drug you can buy in Mexico. 'Roofie' for short."

I want my daddy.

"Max, there aren't going to be any drugs here. We're not even drinking. I'm a good girl."

"I know that. If you weren't, I wouldn't be here. But Chase Doogle asked me if I could get some from 'back home.' I assumed he meant Mexico and asked a few questions."

"Chase would never do that." I laugh more for myself than Max. "Chase's whole future rides on clean living. You must have heard him wrong."

"I followed him. I've seen him with only two girls: Amber Richardson and you." He clears his throat. "Amber seems to make it clear that she's available without pharmaceutical help, so I can only assume—" He looks at my purity ring.

I pull my hands away. "I don't believe you. I've known Chase my whole life! He would never do such a thing. You're just jealous."

"I am jealous. You've known Chase? Or this version of Chase you've created?"

"Stop it. Stop your lying! Why would you do this?"

"I gave him an unmarked Excedrin. If he does try anything, you'll be safe."

I step into the house, slam the door, and lock it behind me.

"Who's that on the porch?" Claire asks as she descends the stairs.

I'm shaking. "Your boss."

"What's he doing here? I didn't invite him early." She tries to see through the glass. "Why don't you let him in?"

"He says he—never mind. You look beautiful, Claire."

She's wearing an LBD (you know, the standard little black dress) with a V-neck lined in silver beading. She has a matching silver headband and a strand of long pearls. "You look like a stunning flapper. The twenties never looked so good."

"It's chiffon." She swivels back and forth so I can see her slender frame. "It feels like heaven. I have to stay away from the barbecue, though, so I don't smell like smoke." She looks out the door. "He's still there. I'll just let him in."

"Don't!" I say, guarding the door. "I don't think he's going away."

"Come on, let's get you dressed. I bought you some temporary blonde highlights for tonight."

"You did?"

She nods. "And a little tiara to go with your dress."

"My dress? I was just going to wear my new jeans and a peasant shirt. What, do I have a fairy godmother tonight?"

"You do," she says as she starts back up the stairs.

"Claire?"

"Yeah?"

"Do you think Chase would ever try anything funny?"

"Well, I hope so. What's this party about anyway?"

"No, I mean, do you think if a girl said no, he'd take that for her answer?"

She stops on the landing. "No to a kiss, or no to something more? Is this about Greg? Look, I know he has a little pyro fetish, but I assure you, he's a complete gentleman. Nothing has ever happened that I should be ashamed of." She looks me squarely in the eye. "Really. He's kissed me, and I've kissed him back, but his parents were home, and he hasn't touched me here. Says it's too dangerous."

"What about Max? Is he what you'd consider honest? Aboveboard?"

"For a Don Juan, he's great." She laughs. "If my father found out I was hosting an Argentine, he'd go ballistic. You know, my father's English. You hear about their soccer rivalry? That's like high treason in this household."

"Yeah. Yeah, their teams don't like each other, I get it."

"The Hand of God play in soccer? Where they stole the World Cup?"

"Oh my gosh, that's right," I say with a sick recognition. "The illegal handball that gave Argentina an unpenalized goal and, ultimately, the World Cup. It's soccer legend."

"And it's our funeral if he comes here in a soccer jersey. But I wouldn't hold even that over Max. He's a peach." She leads me into her bedroom and pulls out a bright pink paisley minidress.

"Oh my goodness, it's gorgeous." I reach out to touch the divine dress. "I don't think my mother has ever touched this fabric before in her life. Can you imagine if she designed dresses like this? I'd be the most popular girl in school." I drop the skirt. "Okay, well, maybe not the most unpopular anyway."

"The color is flamingo. I thought that was a sign. It's a Badgley Mischka halter dress. It will totally make you look like you have boobs." She points to the empire waist. "And look at the Victorian brooch in the antique platinum color. Isn't it perfect? It's so old Hollywood. Perfect for you."

"It is perfect for me, but I'm paying you for it. What do I owe you?"

"I'm not taking your money. You need it for college. I've hired a photographer for tonight, and just in case Chase decides to go on that stupid trip in March, you'll have your cherished photograph."

"How'd you know about that?"

"You've been carrying that prom journal everywhere. Like I'm not going to read it. Please."

"You read my prom journal?" I start to categorize all the pathetic drivel I wrote in it. "Did you think it was pathetic?"

"Well, I totally disagree with everything you said about me, but otherwise, well, it was you. I thought it was very you. You are my best friend, you know?"

I give her a big hug. "Thank you for the dress. It's the most beautiful thing I've ever seen." My mind goes back to what Max said, and suddenly I think about Greg. "Don't drink anything tonight."

"We're not having alcohol, Daisy. I'm not that stupid. If I give a reason for anyone to sue my parents, my dad will be back tomorrow." She laughs. "Now let's get your makeup on before you get into that dress."

I stare out the window while she gets out her magic box. Max's car is still there. Somehow I find his presence comforting. I grab Claire's periwinkle Bible with the lime green flower closure and read a few Psalms while Claire plays Carmindy with my face.

"You're done."

I get up and look in the mirror. "I don't even look like me."

"Is that a good thing?"

"I hope so." I grab up the flamingo chiffon dress and slide into it. Claire zips me up as the man at the gate announces that our first guests are here.

"That must be Sarika and Angie. Take your pick of shoes in my mom's closet. She has enormous feet too. I'll meet you downstairs."

I'm pulled to the window and see Max sitting on a teak bench in the garden. Greg and Chase pull up in Greg's old Volvo. When the two of them get out, Max walks toward them. Words are exchanged, and when Max looks up and sees me, his eyebrows lower. He pokes Chase in the chest and appears to be threatening him.

There's an ominous cloud darkening the dusky sky. All I want to do is curl up with Claire's Bible and pray, and maybe call my mommy, but I think about Gil's words. I need to be independent. It's now or never.

"It's not Sarika and Angie," Claire says. "Oh, and what was that you were asking me about earlier?"

"If you had to trust one or the other, Chase or Max, who would it be?"

She shrugs. "I'd trust them both. We've known Chase forever, and Max . . . well, Max is just good people."

"With Chase, I'll know one way or the other tonight if he wants something to happen or if I'm just a restless puppy at his feet. It's better to know rather than knock myself out for the rest of the year. Right?"

"Daisy." She grabs my shoulders and shakes me. "We're having a party, we're not going to a funeral. Lighten up!"

"Greg is under police surveillance. What if Chase was trying to get him the drug? What if his gentleman thing is all an act?"

"Now you're just talking crazy. He's not under surveillance. He's on probation. There's a difference. I don't think they do stakeouts on every teenage prank gone awry."

"The only difference is they didn't search his garage! Which might come with five to ten if they found the explosives he has in there. He must have them, Claire. Or he wouldn't have known the sugar mix was legal."

"Greg doesn't have explosives."

"I got the same physics assignment. If he was staging his rocket and using propulsion technology—"

"Look at the bright side. He'll be ready for Armageddon when it comes. You really are paranoid, you know. Just like your father. You think everyone is ready to blow up the world. Stock up on Pop Tarts, the end is here!"

"I'm premillennial. As a Christian, why wouldn't I believe I'm going up before the hard stuff starts down here on earth? Since God doesn't say, I'm putting my expectations out there." I spread my arms. "Lord, take me away! I'm ready to fly!"

"I don't know why you don't like Greg. Can we drop it?"

"It's not that I don't like him. I just think he has issues."

"I like people with issues. You're my best friend, right?"

"Snap," I tell her drolly.

"Let's go greet our guests." She pokes at the edges of my lips. "Party face! Party face!"

"I'll be right down." I just want to jot something down before I forget.

Prom Journal
December 3
92 Days until Prom
Fact: Can't think of one. I'm too nervous.

This is my first high school party. I mean, with both boys and girls and no youth pastor present. The fact that Claire and I pulled this off without getting caught gives me a rush of adrenaline. Gil would be proud. I said Claire and I could handle this, and I was right. If the party were to get out of hand, which it won't because there won't be any alcohol, but if it were, I have 9-1-1 speed-dialed into my BlackBerry—which I will keep on my person at all times.

I'm totally responsible. Being a perfectionist has always been beneficial for me, but I have this dark thrill that perhaps I haven't used this trait to its full advantage. I cannot be a social outcast and still maintain safety and a fun environment.

God would be proud, I think.

Okay, maybe not about the party, but in terms of being responsible for safety and kids who were going to party anyway. This provides a fun, fantastic atmosphere for them without alcohol. I am like the senior class mommy.

Chase, although he has avoided me at school, told me in a hushed growl that he would be at the party, and in no uncertain terms that I was to save a dance for him. He's so great! Chase has been verbally assaulted by my father and he's still here. He now knows my freakdom is not simply a mask I wear. Either my lifelong crush has come to an explosive ending, or he'll fight for me. It's one or the other. He'll prove that there's a reason he's won my loyalty for twelve years. Am I ready for the emptiness if he turns me down?

I was thinking maybe I'd been sort of prophetic, letting him kiss me in kindergarten, when all along, it was just a giant setup for disappointment. If Chase isn't the one, I've wasted so much time. So much energy and pain. I can't even bear to think about it. It's like God saying to me, why just go down when you can go down in a ball of flames? Not that God thinks like me.

Maybe being perfect is not possible, but aren't we supposed to strive to be like Jesus? Okay, it's probably a stupid question since I'm dressed like some girl from the Upper East Side and I've lied to my parents to be here.

I get it. I'm not perfect. Maybe Chase isn't either. It's time to find out.

Claire, if you're reading this, mind your own business!

14

"Dinner was incredible, Greg," Claire says.

"He knows his way around a fire." I clear my throat. "I mean, barbecue."

"Why's that guy Max hanging around? You didn't invite him to dinner, did you?" Chase asks.

"He's going to help me play bouncer. In case anyone wants to crash the gate." Lying has become so easy for me. I feel utterly soiled, but I haven't taken my eyes off of Claire's drink.

"The band's setting up. Should we get this party started?" Chase asks, shaking his booty with what I can only describe as white-boy disease. Which, an hour ago, I might have thought cute, but now I'm left disappointed by his moves.

Claire stands up, looking the part of Upper East Side socialite. She's beautiful and, like her mother, knows the way around a hostess table. She's a natural. "I want to talk to Daisy first." She pulls me roughly into the house and stops at the foyer. "Send Max home and cut this out. You've been like a wet dishrag all night. If you can't go through with the party and defy your parents, go home. Max can drive you. Oh wait, no he can't because you can't do that either, can you?"

"Let me talk to Max. I want to get him out of my head."

"He grew up in a country where nothing works right. Of course he's going to be questioning the guys' motives. Drugs, Daisy? Come on, we've known these guys since kindergarten. They wouldn't know how to buy drugs if their lives depended on it."

"Of course they wouldn't, that's why they asked the only Hispanic guy at St. James. Racist and dumb."

"You think Chase is dumb now? I thought you liked him because of his intellect."

I grab my head. "I don't know what to think. I only know I can't get what Max said out of my head. He's got no reason to lie."

"Um, he does have a reason, and you're standing in front of me. Go out and talk to him and tell him to leave. Sarika and Angie will hopefully be here for dessert. Just go." She pushes me toward the door. "I did not play your fairy godmother for you to turn into a wicked stepsister all night!"

She opens the front door and pushes me out. I stumble directly into Max.

"*Bellissima!*"

"Stop it. No Italian."

He holds his hands up. "Sometimes only Italian will do. No one appreciates beauty like the Italians. There's an old saying in Buenos Aires: 'Porteños are Latin Americans who talk like Italians, act like the British, and think they live in Paris.'"

"Enough sweet talk. You have to go." I push against his chest with both hands.

"You look so beautiful, Daisy. That dress was made for you. You were made for dresses. Why do you hide yourself in those pants all the time?"

"You noticed?" I shake my head. "No, you're not lulling me in. I'm leaving."

Sarika and Angie pull up, and I step back from Max. "Hi, gals. Everyone's in back eating. The band is going to start any minute, and then the rest of the people arrive."

"The luminaries look so pretty," Sarika says. She's wearing her full-length Indian sari in a canary yellow with silver and gold beading down the front.

"You look gorgeous, Sarika." I look over at Angie, who's dressed in a tailored sailor dress that fits her snugly and hugs all the right places. "You too, Angie!"

"Are we *Gossip Girl*?" Angie asks.

"How would I know? I can't watch it either."

Max opens the door for them, bowing at the waist. "She'll be right with you."

I try to act flustered with Max's defiance, but the truth is, it's hard to walk away from someone who seeks you out like he does. This would make a great life lesson about God if I weren't spending my whole night totally pretending at a party that shouldn't be happening.

"Go on, Max. Leave or come join the party. I'll watch out for her."

"For who?"

"Chase must have asked you about the . . . you know . . . for Greg. Maybe he's tired of playing the gentleman with Claire. I'll make certain nothing happens."

Max frowns. "I'm not wrong. Is that what you think? You think I'm going to accuse someone of trying to buy a drug off me, which by the way is extremely offensive, as if all Hispanics are drug dealers!" He stops to let me assess the craziness of the situation. "Do you think I want to tell the girl I desire for myself that her crush thinks I'm a drug dealer?"

"I just meant Chase wouldn't—" I stop. "What did you just say?"

"I know I look like a jerk. I get it. No one wants me here. You think it's easy to stand out here on the porch, knowing no one wants me here? Ask yourself." He holds me at the arms. "Why would I be here if it weren't true?"

"You don't look like a drug dealer. You look like an Argentine model who starred as Nacho."

He offers the dregs of a smile and my heart breaks. I want to tell myself there's nothing here, that I don't feel anything for Max, but instinctively I know that isn't true, and I feel every bit the betrayer. I had my mind set. Chase is my date. Chase is the man I've always loved, and yet, so easily, my heart could be swayed by another. What kind of true love is that?

"You're trying to put doubt in my mind." I bounce my finger at him. "I have to admit, it's a very good plan, and it would probably work if I didn't know Chase so well. I barely know you, Max. You're a stranger to me."

"You know him because he sat in the same school for all these years?"

"Precisely."

He shrugs. "Then go back to your Prince Charming. I'm happy to be wrong, but he did try to buy the drug from me, and he did take it when offered."

"Wait a minute. You gave him the drug?"

Max rolls his eyes. "Didn't I tell you? Where would I get a roofie? I slipped him an unmarked Excedrin. If he puts it in your drink, it won't melt. A roofie melts."

My eyes narrow at him. "Thanks for the information."

"I looked it up on the internet before I gave him the Excedrin. I didn't know. I sell hot dogs."

"I know that."

"Go enjoy your party. You look incredible. I like"—he waves his hand over his head—"you know, the blonde. I'm probably not supposed to notice that, huh? It's like a woman's age. I have so far to go."

I stand beside him, pausing for some unknown reason. "Max, come on. Come with me. You can teach us how to tango." I grab his hand, and he pulls me closer, pushing me into tango pose, which causes me to giggle.

"You are not ready to tango. First, you must learn the steps. It's a circle, then you move with intention." He stretches out my arm. "It is all in the attitude. Look at me. Give me some attitude."

I try to muster all the attitude I can, but I'm worried I look more like I have a stomachache.

He laughs.

"You are way too smooth for me, Max. Sophisticated. Isn't that what you like to say? You are way too sophisticated for the likes of me."

He starts leading me again in his dance. "Do you feel my right hand?" He places it on my upper back. "This is how I lead. You follow my hand—when I push, you turn."

"Like a puppet?"

"Uh, no. A puppet has no intention. When you learn the steps, you follow my 'chest intention.' You won't even need the hand."

"I think this is illegal."

"You have watched too much *Dancing with the Stars*. First

you learn the steps. Right." He pushes me backward. "Left, right, left, promenade." I stumble over his foot. "Try again. Right, left, right, left, pivot."

"I'm terrible."

"You are, but you'll get better. Give me some attitude. Slow, slow, quick, quick, pivot. Wrap your leg around the back of my knee."

We try the dance again, and I end up hanging like a limp rag doll. He lifts me close, and my heart is pounding at his proximity. "You have to learn to trust your partner. If you don't let me lead, it is not the tango." He lets go of me suddenly. "I doubt your band knows any tango. I am not smooth, I am utterly entranced."

"Stop it." I giggle, my hands on his chest. The chemistry between us is natural, but not because he's any more velvet teddy bear than the next guy. We get each other. "You're going to stand out here on the porch instead of coming and dancing with me? That's weird. You're pulling a tantrum."

"A what?"

"You heard me, you're acting like a toddler who doesn't get his way."

He pushes me away. "Go to your party, *Bellissima*. I will throw no more tantrums." He raises his hand. "If you don't check in with me every hour on the hour, I'm coming to get you." His black T-shirt stretches across his perfectly toned body, and I force my eyes away.

"When I met you that first day, you seemed so unsure of yourself, so happy to meet me as a friend. To be known. But that's not you at all, is it? You were playing me."

"Just because I do things differently doesn't make me a dog. The truth will bear out, and unlike your friend, I can wait." He leans against the brick wall, crossing his arms and his feet at the ankles.

"What are you studying when you get back to Argentina? Are you going to be the next Bruno Tonioli?" I ask, referring to the Italian, overly expressive judge on *Dancing with the Stars*.

"Hasn't Claire told you?"

"Believe it or not, you don't fill our conversations."

"I should." He grins. "I'm going to be a pastor."

My cheek muscles tighten. "You are not!"

"What is so funny about that?"

"We're not allowed to dance in my church. You're going to be a tango-loving pastor?"

"You cannot live in Argentina and not know how to tango. It is a national necessity, but my country, like yours, is in desperate need of revival."

I back away from him. "My dad sent you. That's why I can't trust you. This is all a big joke to you, isn't it?"

He holds his hand on his heart. "I pledge that I have never met your father. Other than that day he took the stage at school, and I don't know, I wouldn't call that a meeting."

The front door opens. "Everything okay out here?" Chase stands there and grins. He came to my rescue. I gaze at him, then back at Max.

"Everything's fine."

Chase holds up a bottle. "I stole some bubbly from my dad. Come share with us. I thought we'd celebrate my future."

"Where'd you get that?" I try to grab the bottle, but he whisks it away. "Chase, we said nothing illegal at this party."

"Champagne isn't illegal."

"It is if you're seventeen. Give me that."

He shuts the door but winks at me first.

"Did you see that? That was the most cheese-ball move I've ever seen. He did not do that." I pace the front porch. "I've got bugs crawling all over me."

Max is laughing. "Next thing you know, you're starring in a cheesy rock video and writhing around on the beach in your Christian bikini."

"This is not funny." I drop my head. "I'm a poseur. Look at this dress. I'm a poseur. I've got to go keep this party under control. You know, I always think I can handle Claire, but that's not true. She always throws me a curveball."

"That's not Claire. That's life, Daisy."

I meet Max's dark, serious eyes. If there's deceit in them, I am blind to all of it. I can hear the party getting louder, but I'm not wooed by it. I'm more interested in knowing why Max came tonight. Why he's willing to stay on the front porch, in the background.

"Do you think I'm not capable of handling things? Is that why you're here?" I ask him in an almost accusatory tone.

"I'm here because God told me I should be. I suppose I'll find out." He raises his brows mysteriously.

"Maybe I should wait and find out with you." I step a bit closer to him. "Do you think?"

He grins, and I feel warmed by his presence. Safe. "I'd be honored if you would."

I sink to the porch steps and pat the bricks beside me. Max sits beside me, and I can feel his leg touching my own. We talk about everything, from international politics to our rap names, well into the evening. Time seems to stand still.

Kids come. Some I recognize, some I don't. The night slips away quietly.

❧ 15 ❧

The roar of the party reaches a fever pitch, and I look at my watch. "Max, it's midnight!" My dress catches on the brick as I pull myself away.

He shrugs. "Do you turn into a pumpkin now?"

"I said I'd watch out for Claire! I have to go check on her. How did it get to be so late?"

He looks out across the driveway and the massive parking lot that's replaced the brick path. "I didn't do a very good job as sentinel either. I'm sorry, I was supposed to help you."

"I'm sure everything's fine. I'm just going to check." I run through the house, which is now a mess. There are pillows on the wood floors, popcorn kernels on the marble, and empty plastic cups everywhere. It's like I've been asleep and I've suddenly awoken to a very bad nightmare.

Max and I talked about his dreams, my dreams, and the reality that stops them from coming true. He promised to pray for me. I promised to pray for him, but the underlying current between us made me question everything I'd thought to be true about Chase. What if I wasn't meant to have one true love?

I feel a strong sense of calm and hear a resonant voice in

my soul. *You WERE meant to have one true love, Daisy. It's not Max or Chase.* I hear it as though it were spoken directly to me, and I know my conscience is seething.

I walk through the house, opening all the closed doors. Sometimes I find couples clutched together; another room has a group of guys playing beer pong on a skateboard. "Get out of here!" I hear myself shout. They scatter like rats. In the giant foyer, someone has taken toilet paper and threaded it through the curved bannister, and it waves in the breeze from the front door. All I can think about is how laughable my perfectionism seems now. How void my vision of maturity currently seems.

The majority of kids are still in the backyard, and the band's music forces the talking levels to screaming. At the sight, I know I have to call the police. I need help, and all I can think of is that joke about how you eat an elephant one bit at a time.

I scour the crowd, searching for Claire, but she's nowhere in sight amid the throng of kids. The yard is massive, and yet it's inundated with throbbing, sweaty bodies, some clad only in bikini tops and skirts—which is disturbing considering this is supposed to be a Christian party. Most of the guys are wearing screened T-shirts and skinny jeans or plaid shorts, but some of them—those with six-pack abs, it seems—are shirtless. The shapes and colors mix and swirl into a giant canvas of bodies. Bodies, I think with terror, I've never seen before in my life.

The grassy area is used as a dance floor, with the brick Tudor pool house serving as a stage for the band, which I'd describe as a mix of AC/DC and Jonas Brothers. I wonder where Claire found them—how any of this happened, really.

It seems impossible that our small seedling of a party, in order to get noticed by our classmates, could have erupted into this. My eyes and ears will probably never recover, and the thought of having fun in this kind of chaos is ridiculous. All I can think about is Claire's parents and the house they've worked so hard for, the precious treasures they've filled it with, and I feel so ungrateful. All the times they fed me, took me on family trips, and this is how I repay them—with a yard full of gyrating strangers.

The swimming pool in the middle of the yard is full as well, with people dancing to the beat in their own watercise class. The food in the outdoor kitchen and patio has been picked over, and there's nothing left but bits of parsley and chicken bones, along with a banged-up keg next to the smoking barbecue. No sustenance.

"You made it!" Chase wanders toward me in a crisscross pattern, and I can't tell if he's drunk or pretending to be. The bottle of champagne is in his hand, and he lifts it in some kind of toast. Our *Gossip Girl* theme looks more like *Animal House*.

I clutch my BlackBerry in my hand. One call to the police and this will all be over. Claire will kill me, but that's probably the best of my options. I close my eyes in the middle of the ruckus and pray for an answer, then Chase barrels into me clumsily. I push him off me.

"What are you doing?" I shout.

"Come on, Daisy. Let's celebrate," he slurs. "We're going to be off to college and these lazy days of high school will all be over." He whips the bottle around as he speaks. Something tells me it's not the first one he's emptied. "Well?" He comes close to my face, the sour smell of alcohol on his breath.

"They're all over. I get trained. I'm off to war and I might never see you again." He nuzzles into my neck, looks up at me with his hazel eyes wide, and puckers his lower lip. "You wouldn't want that to happen, would you, Daisy May? My sweet Daisy May Crispin. I love your name. It's so sweet. Girl next door. But come on, Daisy. I bet you're not so shy. Huh, Daisy?"

"Where's Claire?"

"Claire's celebrating! Let's go celebrate." He drops the empty bottle. "You know, your boyfriend tried to sell me an Excedrin instead of a roofie. What does he think I am, some kind of idiot?"

I get a sinking feeling in the pit of my stomach. My heart stops for a moment as I realize Max told me the truth. How could I have questioned it? He came to the party and never left the front porch for us.

"What's a roofie?" I ask in my best innocent voice.

He laughs. "It's a relaxing pill. You know, for people who have a hard time relaxing. They're perfect for high-strung people like us." He slides to the grass. "I need to sit down." He pulls me down beside him. "You sit down too."

My dress, already having been pulled from the brick, will now have mud spots and grass stains. "There's nothing more disgusting than a drunk person," I say.

"See? Too high-strung. You need to relax. Relax with me, Daisy."

"You're drunk, Chase."

"Come on. Give me a fact, Daisy. Tell me something about drunk people. You know any facts about drunk people?"

"I know they're ridiculous. Where's Claire?" I stand up and brush off the back of my dress.

"I told you, she's with Greg. They're celebrating." He lies back with his head on the patio and his legs on the grass, and bodies gyrate over him on the makeshift dance floor. There's a sea of kids, and I don't recognize any of them. They're all wearing casual shorts and ripped T-shirts, that type of thing. I feel panic as I search for a familiar face.

"Sarika!" I see her near the pool with Angie. "Angie!" I wave, running toward them. Both of them look like they've been pegged by a laser.

"We called the police," Angie says. "We're going home."

"Where's Claire?" I ask them.

"She was hanging all over Greg. That's the last time we saw her." Sarika shakes her head. "You were supposed to watch out for her."

"I didn't know it would get like this," I yell over the crowd. I look to the outdoor kitchen. Two guys built like linebackers are throwing the empty keg around in anger. It crashes on top of the grill, and the dent it makes is substantial.

Then life happens as if in slow motion. I hear myself yell, "Noooo!"

I run to close the sparking barbecue as the empty keg crashes into the nearby gas line. I push the guys away, but fire erupts almost immediately and climbs the vine and wooden trellis, igniting the corner of the house. Then the sirens begin. Thank goodness Sarika and Angie had the sense of mind to call. *Why didn't I do this? Where is my sensible brain? My designated-driver soul?*

"Why didn't I do this?"

Chase curses. "The cops! I gotta get out of here!" His slurring has evaporated, and he runs like the wind. I'm stunned as I see the back of him getting smaller in the distance.

My hero is a complete zero. It can't be true.

"Where's Claire?" I ask everyone I pass, but they're all running to get away from the house. I lift up my dress to cover my face and nose and enter the house. I'm pulled from behind.

"No, Daisy." Max pulls me out of the house. "I'll go. Where's her room?"

"In the front, where you saw me from earlier!"

The band has stopped, and they do their best to get their instruments far from the house. The yard is nothing more than garbage, empty cans floating in the pool.

The gas line is still open, and the fire quickly engulfs the whole side of the house. I run to search for the shut-off valve. My dad always taught me to get out of the house and go for the shut-off valve. I run around the house, looking for the red valve that is so easily marked at my own house, but I see nothing like it.

As I watch the flames lick the edge of the house, I have visions of an explosion and I am frantic to find the line. In my head, I recite prayer after prayer. *Please, Lord, get us out of here alive. Nothing else matters. Get us out of here alive.*

Greg and Claire come running out of the house together. Claire catches sight of the flames at the edge of the house, and her face turns stone cold.

"Where's Max? He went in looking for you!" I shake her shoulders. "Where's Max, Claire?" I'm feeling frenzied by now as an upstairs window blows out, followed by a flash of flame. The roof has caught now, and the flames are well into the sky.

I run around the house and am met by a line of firemen. "Max is in the house," I yell, panting for breath. "My friend

Max. He went inside. In that room there! That's where he went. Please!" I scream. "Please, get him out!" One of the firemen pushes me out of the way, and I watch as men in full gear head into the house. Just then Max staggers out of the house with a girl in his arms and collapses on the lawn. Two of the firemen immediately go to work, and I stand by, screaming out prayers. I think I'm hysterical. I just hear my own cries as I struggle for breath.

"You're burned," a firefighter says to me.

"No, I'm not burned. Get Max. Please!"

"Come with me," the fireman says. He tries to put me on a stretcher, but I protest. "Max!"

Max, still unconscious, lies flat on the front porch while I'm led away. The girl who was in his arms rouses. It's Amber Richardson. They load her into the ambulance with me, her blonde hair splayed in a sunshine pattern on the ambulance bed. It's not the pretty sight I'd once imagined.

I never imagined I'd be in this position. I never imagined that Claire's bright idea for a party might lead to this. I'm left to dwell on my lack of perfection as I watch the casualties of my mistakes.

I'm sorry, Lord.

I think I say something about roofies to the fireman, and it's my last memory.

❧ 16 ❧

"Daisy!" I hear my mother's voice. "She's awake!! Doctor, she's awake!"

"Too loud," I hear myself moan. "Shut up." Now, I have never told my mom to shut up in my life, and I'm in this twilight state, so I can't tell if I said it aloud or not.

"Daisy, what a terrible thing to say!"

I said it out loud.

"But I'm so glad you said something. You were in shock, so they put you under for the pain. Do you feel any pain?"

"What pa—" I don't even get the word out. "My wrist!"

"You've got third-degree burns, but only on a very small part. Most of them are second-degree, but that's what hurts," my mom says. "The kids at the party said you saved a lot of lives by shutting off the gas valve."

"Couldn't find it." I shake my head. "I didn't—"

"Couldn't find what, honey?"

"Water," I tell her. She holds a cup up to my lips, and I sip the cool water.

"The police want to talk with you when you're ready," the doctor says.

"No, not yet," Mom says. "I told them later." My mom bus-

200

ies her hands by moving the blankets around my feet. Just her slight action induces so much guilt. That's the thing about having the Holy Spirit. You can't get away with much, not without conscience anyway. Everything is permissible, but not everything is beneficial. Don't I know it. "You shut the barbecue lid."

"Claire?"

"Claire's fine, honey. She wasn't hurt. She won't be fine when her mother gets home, but for now, she's fine. She's going to be staying with us until her mom flies in tonight. Her dad is still trying to get a plane."

"Max?" I croak.

"I haven't heard about him." Mom puts her hand on my hip gently. "Is he a friend of yours?"

My hand is throbbing, and though it's loosely wrapped, I can feel a blistering wound underneath. "Where's Dad?"

My mom doesn't say anything. "Are you feeling all right, Daisy? They gave you something to help with the pain."

I look at my hand. "It hurts."

"Second-degree burns hurt more than third, apparently. They don't kill the nerve endings. Luckily, you have third-degree only in a very small area. That's great, isn't it?"

I laugh. "Now who is giving the facts?"

My mother starts to sob in her hands. "What were you doing, Daisy?"

"Why isn't Dad here?"

She busies herself with pillows, walks around the room, and finally sits down next to me. "I haven't told him yet."

I swallow hard. "Why not?"

"Because his baby girl, whom he has worked so hard to protect, doesn't appear to value the life she's been given enough to act responsibly."

"Excuse us, Mom," a nurse says. "We need to check and dress the wound. Would you please wait outside?"

My mom gives me that look that makes me want to scream, but the simple act of the nurse moving the wrap on my hand causes it instead.

My mom is there in a second, and when she looks at my hand, she starts to bawl. "Daisy! No!"

The nurse escorts her out the door again while another one smiles sweetly at me. "You got off lucky, you know."

"Is Max Diaz here? Is he all right?"

"I'll have to check for you. We're giving you fluids to replace anything lost. Your blood pressure looks great, though."

"Is this going to scar?" I ask, looking at the oozing, pale skin.

"Probably," she says. "But you were so fortunate."

"I feel so weak."

"That's your body healing. I'll let you rest, and I'll send your mom back in."

After a few minutes, the curtain pulls back and shuts again. Claire is standing beside me. "Oh my gosh, Daisy. I thought you were dead or something. What are you doing to me?"

I laugh, which makes me hurt more, and I laugh again. "Only you would blame me for this. I was on the porch, having a lovely time dancing the tango with a hot Argentine who looks like Taco, and you—you were throwing a keg party."

"You're not making any sense."

"Nacho," I say. "He looks like Nacho. Have you seen Max?"

She shakes her head, with that sad look people give you when they don't want to tell you bad news.

202

"If you know something, you'd better tell me."

"I promise, I don't know anything. Amber Richardson is alive and well. Never thought I'd be happy to hear myself say that, but I am."

"Did you talk to your mother?"

"No, but I listened to her quite a bit. She's on her way home now. So's my dad."

"I blame you for this. If you hadn't numbed yourself with all that shopping, you would have been fine with going with me and soothing yourself. How many times have I shadowed you at the mall, lusted over what you've bought, and come home totally empty-handed, and now, in my time of need, where were you? Getting a job at the wiener barn and planning a *Gossip Girl* gig." I shake my head. "I knew when you started playing terrorist with Greg in his front yard that you were up to no good." I exhale. "Normal people don't blow things up in their front yards."

"I blew it."

"What's your house look like?"

"Like we had a barbecue." She laughs. "Oh, Daisy, I am so sorry. I never should have gotten you involved in this. Now you're going to be under house arrest until you're thirty. We probably won't graduate with our class, and Amber's hair didn't even get singed."

"It had to happen. At some point my parents were going to find out I'm not perfect. Why not have it be in a blaze of glory? Literally." I grab her hand with my good one. "Go find out about Max. He went back in the house to get Amber." Recognition hits me like another flame. "Chase left. He just left." The shock I feel is incredible. "He was my hero. How could I have it all wrong? All these years?"

"He hasn't had basic training yet. Maybe he'll learn something about being a hero after that."

"He's no hero. Not to me. All the emotion I've wasted—"

The curtain snaps back, and my mother stands there. "Claire, sit down. I need to talk to both of you."

I swallow all thoughts of wasted emotion. Something tells me I'm going to need to save some strength for this talk: a verbal beating to conquer all sermons.

Claire sits down as she's told. Her dress is a wreck, and we both smell like a fireplace. The painful reminder of our evening, and what disasters we are on our own, rushes through my head.

"Daisy's father can't take this kind of stress," my mother begins. "It's going to break his heart, so I haven't told him yet."

Here we go. "It would stress me out to dress as a pirate with mutton chops and rap too. You know? This isn't all our fault."

My mom is quiet. She pets her own hand like a lap dog, takes a moment, and then starts again. "Your father had a series of small strokes a few years back, Daisy. He's not the same as he once was."

"Mom, I feel guilty, all right! You're going to make something up to make me feel worse? What more can I do, Mom? I screwed up, I know it!"

My mom, who never yells, snaps, "Listen, Daisy! You are acting like a spoiled brat! Did you hear what I said? Your father could have taken you out of that school when he lost his permanent job after the strokes, but he didn't. He did whatever he could to put food on the table. He couldn't drive at night, so he knelt by his chair every night until you came home safely.

This is how you repay him! You make fun of him, you laugh behind his back, you have no respect! What's the one thing the Bible asks of you as a child? To obey your parents, and you can't even do that!" She sobs again, but her scowl returns. "You think you know it all, don't you, Daisy? You're too good for the likes of us!" She storms out of the room.

Claire blinks repeatedly. "Your dad had a stroke?" she asks.

I blink away the tears. "No, she's just making it up." I shake the thought away. "Don't you think?"

Claire shakes her head slowly. "I don't think so. Your mom doesn't lie, and I can't imagine she'd lie about that."

I think back to the wad of cash my mother gave me for clothes, and it occurs to me that my parents are total strangers to me. My dad, the man who always has everything under control and never lets anything ruffle his feathers, had a stroke. It's almost too much to digest. But for some reason my thoughts go back to that foreign wad of cash and the realization that my parents harbor a separate, inner world not discernible from my vantage point, which makes me question everything.

"I wonder where she got that money."

"I don't know." Claire shakes her head. "I may have burned my parents' house down, and I'd still rather be me right now."

"Ever the supportive one," I tell her. "I seared my flesh for you." I hold up my arm and moan. "Go find out about Max. I have life to digest. I'm a terrible, miserable person."

"Aren't we all?" She pats me on the knee and leaves. I close my eyes and picture my father praying for me on the side of his beat-up chair.

"I am a spoiled brat," I tell the wired ceiling. "I get it, all right?"

"Are you talking to me?" An older nurse has come in. "Your blood pressure is doing well, so let's not get upset."

"The guy I loved was a figment of my imagination, the guy I could love is MIA, my dad is disabled, I helped burn my friend's house down, and the back of my wrist is burned, probably scarred forever. What's to get upset about?"

"Oh, honey, at your age everything feels dramatic."

I stare at the nurse with my mouth open. I'm sure something on the list passes the realm of your standard drama queen. Maybe it's me, but . . .

My mom comes back in the room. The green of her eyes is illuminated by the transparent red around them, and her nose is bulbous and pink. Great, more guilt.

"Mom?"

"I'm sorry I lost my temper," she says.

"No, I deserved it."

She searches the room, looks everywhere but at me. What I'd give for one of those shaming looks at the moment. I mean, I finally deserve it! "Why didn't you tell me about Dad?"

"One day when you're older, you'll understand how important a man's pride is to him."

"Is he all right?"

"He's fine. He has residual symptoms, that's all. You have your studies to worry about. We didn't want to alarm you."

"Mom, that's alarming. My dad had a stroke. Claire's parents are divorcing. Her house caught on fire. Sometimes life is alarming."

"I want you to live carefree as a child. These are adult concepts." She still hasn't looked at me. "You know, he doesn't see as well. His mind gets a bit slow when he's tired."

"You should have told me."

"I probably should have," she admits. She finally looks at me. For a split second. "I found your friend Max."

Of all things, I feel his right hand on my back, leading me. "Is he all right?"

Her head snaps up. "He's being monitored. He had smoke inhalation."

"Monitored? What does that mean?"

"I don't want you to have to keep your dad's secret, Daisy, but I don't want you to treat him with kid gloves either. He would hate that."

"Mom, what about Max?"

"I don't know, honey. I know the police are waiting to talk to him. Did you know there were drugs at the party? And alcohol?" My mother shakes her head. "I know you had nothing to do with that. I told the police that. You had nothing to do with that, right?"

"No," I tell her.

"That Amber girl, the one you've never gotten along with very well—do you remember when she threw your collectible Barbie down the sewer?"

I nod. My mom doesn't remember that Claire proceeded to throw Amber down the sewer after the doll. She never did ask how I got the filthy doll back.

"That girl was such a mean one. Do you know she stuck her tongue out at me in preschool Sunday school when I taught? Preschool!"

"Mom, what about Amber?"

"Well," my mother says, coming closer, "it appears she was drugged. I cannot believe you were even at a party where a girl was drugged! Daisy, what were you thinking?"

"Chase."

"Chase is fine. He's at home. He wasn't at the party, was he?"

"He drugged her!"

"Oh no, honey. Chase wasn't there. It appears she came down with that boy you're asking about."

"He went in to get her, Mom. I sent him in after Claire!"

"You sent someone into a fire? Daisy, you know better than that."

"Well, I do now! He went in, Mom. I couldn't stop him."

"Of course you couldn't."

"Mom." I force her to look at me by pausing.

"What?"

"Chase tried to buy drugs off Max."

"Is Max a drug dealer?"

I bang my head against the pillow. "Never mind."

"I'm going to drop Claire off at home. I suppose I'll have to tell your father what the two of you have been up to." She stands up and brushes her dress down.

"Mom, you're so thin."

She twists a bit. It's the closest my mother will ever get to vanity. "Forty-five pounds."

"I've been so busy, I haven't really noticed how much it was—not until I saw you dance. I couldn't believe you could actually dance again, Mom."

"I have reason to dance, sweetheart. My family is alive and well."

She shrugs, and it makes me sad. She's used to not being noticed, that's the truth of the matter, and the fact that I've ignored her as much as everyone else has makes me see a truth in myself I do not want to face.

"Is there anything I can get for you from home?" Her eyes well up with tears. "I'm sorry I've made you wear those clothes," she says. "I wanted you to be loved for you, not your fashion sense."

"Mom, what's the matter?"

"You're a good girl."

"I'm not perfect."

She laughs. "Did you think we were under the delusion that you were?"

"I think you expected it, yes."

My mother nods. She appears resigned.

"Did you hear me?"

"I heard you," she says. She faces me and unties the macramé knot on top of her purse. (Yeah, I know.) She pulls out a wad of cash.

"What's this?"

"It's your tuition for college. Do you think I'm perfect, Daisy?"

"Not if I go by your handbag choice. Absolutely not." I count the money. "This is six hundred and seventy-five dollars. Where did you get this?"

"Put it away." She pushes the cash down on the bed. I hand it back to her, and she wraps it in the hammock moonlighting as a purse. "I earned it, it's legal."

"I know it's legal. Why do you have it?"

"Your father isn't very good with money. If I don't hide it, he spends it."

"You hide money from Dad?"

"He's a good man, your dad."

"Mom—"

She leans in and whispers, "We don't have health insurance

210

at the moment. I couldn't make that payment and the house payment. I chose the roof over our head. That's what Dave Ramsey says to do."

I notice she has a waist. My mother has a waist. I realize it's an odd thing to note at the time of hearing we have no health insurance, but it's such a testimony to who my mother is. She fought to get herself a waist, and she did, even though she never seems to leave her sewing machine or my dad's side.

"How will we pay for this?" I stammer.

"That's just it. I'm not certain, honey. But Jehovah-Jireh will provide. He always does."

"What about focusing on the inside?" I feel a little betrayed. "You said if you focused on cleaning the inside, God would take care of the outside, but look at what's happened. We can't take care of the outside or the inside, for that matter."

"I did focus on the inside. That's how I lost the weight. I asked God why I overate, and I'm treating my body like a temple." My mother, whose long, dark hair is usually in a sloppy ponytail, has a hairstyle—with what looks like a bump-it on the back.

"Who are you? And what did you do with my mother?"

"There's a lot you haven't taken the time to notice. You're so worried about your makeup and your social life and your *prom date*. There's an entire world functioning around you. Look up once in a while." She touches my chin and lifts it so I look her in the eye. "You might be surprised at what you see." She cinches her purse. "I've got to get home and tell Dad what's happened. He had a late job." She stops. "Oh, and don't mention the insurance. Your dad gets so worried about money."

211

"Yeah." I mean, I would have asked her about the insurance, but I didn't think there was any way she'd go along with it.

She turns back toward me one last time. "You know the costumes I make your father?"

"Sure."

"I've been making aprons of polished cotton and French oil cloth. I've got a pirate, French maids, princesses . . . oh, and a turtle." Her voice trails off.

"You sell them?"

"Well, the children's sizes are thirty-five dollars and the adult sizes are forty-five to sixty dollars, depending on the style. They're for women who entertain and want to let their friends believe they actually cooked for them."

"Sixty dollars! For an apron?"

"You know those women with the big, fancy kitchens? Like Claire's mom? They hire a catering truck."

I know because *Claire* hired a catering truck. I don't know what scares me more—the idea of my mother making money, or the idea of her noticing that she's not dressed like others.

"It's like my whole life's been a lie," I say.

"We just tried to shield you from the hard parts. Your father and I took so much on for our own parents. We didn't want you to have to deal with adult things until you had to. I guess we were off on our timing."

"Mom, my wrist hurts. Can you have them give me something?"

She looks at her purse.

"I'll pay to get the insurance back up, Mom."

"I hadn't thought about what it was like to wear homemade clothes to school. I'd forgotten how difficult kids can be at your age."

"Does Dad know about the aprons?"

She's quiet for a moment. "I'll tell him when the time is right. I've paid off a couple bills. Someday he'll notice that the bills are not piling up, and we'll talk then."

A nurse walks in with a clipboard. "Daisy? Are you Daisy?"

I nod.

"You're a friend of Max Diaz?"

"Yes! Is Max all right?"

She writes something on her clipboard. "He's fine," she says as though discussing an inanimate object. "Is it true you were with him the entire night?"

I look at my mother. "Excuse me, are you a nurse?"

"I work with the hospital's legal department," she says. "Were you with Max Diaz all evening?"

I nod. "I was. We were on my friend's front porch. The whole night!"

"Did you ever see him with anyone else? Alone?"

"He wasn't with anyone!"

"Don't get excited, just formality." She hikes the clipboard under her arm. "Considering ongoing investigations, we would prefer that you not speak with Mr. Diaz or Miss Richardson until the police have had a chance for questioning." She takes out a business card from her pocket. "Call me if you have any questions."

"Questions about what?" my mother asks. "You didn't say anything."

The woman gives a tight-lipped smile. "Thanks for your time."

Prom Journal
January 4
Days until Prom: Who Cares?
Chance of Being Forgotten by St. James Academy: 0
Fact: Fire purifies.

No one will listen. When Max said he was virtually unknown at St. James, he wasn't lying. I told the police
that he was nowhere near Amber. He was with me the
whole night, and don't think that didn't cost me something
with my father, because it did!

Amber doesn't remember anything about the night. She
doesn't remember who gave her the drink, but Chase sure
remembers the unmarked Excedrin. Incidentally, he said
nothing about asking for a pill. The way he looks at me in
the hall, I feel dirty that I ever allowed myself to believe
he had a sense of decency underneath that smooth exterior.

I don't want to even go to prom, but if I did, the only
guy I'd consider going with is currently out of St. James
and my life altogether. (Probably a good move on his part
since I think I may be toxic.) My interlude with international love was brief.

The school said they wouldn't prosecute if he left
quickly, and though they had absolutely nothing on him,
he's here on a student visa. Amber's here as a senator's
daughter and, let's face it, with money.

214

One always wants to believe a Christian school is above such things, but I suppose that's ignorance. Max didn't have to be Einstein to do the math there, and he, the hero of the night, left as though he'd done something wrong. He fired Claire from her hot-dog job, and he won't speak to me. Apparently, neither will his father, because Mr. Diaz hangs up on me too. I know they think I could have fixed this, and I wonder every day myself if that's true. I think I liked being a perfectionist rather than an absolute failure. I should have stuck with that.

What bothers me most is that I thought Max would have fought for me, for the truth. How could he have just stayed quiet and gone away without a fight? Every night, I stare up at my ceiling, and I wonder if he thinks the same thing about me. Why didn't I fight harder for him?

My mom was right. It's worse to have regrets than be forgotten. How I wish I could go back to that life of relative obscurity. Where no one knew my name, sure, but no one followed it up with a snide remark either. Well, with the exception of Amber and Britney, and their names and remarks have only gotten uglier.

Claire and I were allowed to stay at school, but we might as well have been kicked out, for the way we've been treated. I suppose we deserve a good part of it. Amber could have died, the scars from my burns will never fully heal, and worse yet, neither will those on my heart.

As for our popularity, we're known now. But in the same way Carrie was known for going to the prom. We're pariahs who tried to take out the popular kids. There's no actual reason we're to blame, but we're easy targets, I suppose. Claire's romance with Greg is over, and we're back to eating lunch on the lawn in obscurity.

❧ 18 ❧

January 7
The Winter of My Discontent

I thought school was chilly before—you know, frosty at best. But that was before I'd been held accountable for practically barbecuing its leader. It's not just across the PE, though. Our own friends abandoned Claire and me. We're not even welcome in the geek crowd. See? Be careful what you wish for, right?

I keep hearing that old quote from *An Affair to Remember*: "Winter must be cold for those with no warm memories." Seriously? I always hated that part of the movie, like Deborah Kerr was so poetic and Cary Grant should be whisked away by her romanticism. But those of us on the nerd side— especially those of us who share facts like that regularly— well, we know. We know that Cary Grant doesn't fall in love immediately and want to marry you. The truth is, when you spout random facts as conversation starters, people stare at you as if you're babbling aloud to yourself. That's the truth! *Winter is what? Girl, you are cracked!* That's what they're really thinking. *Do you take medication for that?*

I'll never understand it. I mean, why is it socially acceptable to show up to a Christian high school party and sneak a keg in without invitation, but if I happen to mention drunk-driving statistics in that same conversation, I'm the one without a clue. Hey, I happen to know that I wouldn't want to be on that curvy road with half of the students even when they're stone-cold sober. But I'm the idiot. Go figure.

❧ ■ ❧

"The good news," Claire says as we get ready for school at my house, "is that your dad understands you. He trusts you now."

It's a bad day when Claire is the voice of optimism. At least I can avoid some humiliation by getting dropped off in her mother's Lexus, versus the washed-out purple Pontiac.

"I bet he'd let you take a date to prom now—without him being there." She frowns.

I scowl at her. "I bet you could stay home too, if . . . oh wait, you do."

"Touché."

"Girls, you need to get moving," Mrs. Webber says. "You're going to be late. Claire, your father will be back again today. He quit his teaching stint." With her tone she implies that has something to do with us. "So I'm going to pick you both up right after school. Daisy, I'll take you to work, and Claire, you're going to come home and help Mrs. Crispin make dinner."

"Make dinner?"

"Get in the car, you two. We're going to be late, and I have a ton to do before your father gets home."

Claire raises her brows. "You do? Mom, it's good to have you back. I missed you."

By the way she says it, I know she doesn't mean her mother's physical presence. Claire's mother checked out emotionally long before she left the state. Now she sounds like Claire's mother again. All business. There's a comfort for both of us in her drill-sergeant voice.

"We're going to put the house on the market, so I need to check how the repairs are coming."

"We are?" Claire says. "Where are we moving? So Dad's not coming back to us? Just to town?"

"Well, you're going to college. Your father and I are still deciding between jobs."

"Does that mean he's—you're—"

"We can't afford to divorce after the fire and the lawsuits, so for now we're giving it another go."

"How romantic," Claire says.

Yeah, I slapped her.

It's been weird watching Claire's mother become like a real mom again. She helps carpool, she cooks, she's even cleaned up our house so it looks like a "normal people" house. I never noticed how good she is at maintaining order. I always noticed her beauty and the way she twinkled through life like a shooting star, but I missed out on the skill set she'd acquired in doing so. While my mother has heart and undying, sacrificial love for those around her, Mrs. Webber does too, but it's in a different format. My mother is a Mac and Mrs. Webber is a PC. They are both efficient, but in different ways. And Mrs. Webber is cooler.

I never thought having more supervision would fix the problem in our house, but go figure. You know, I think everyone should have houseguests all the time. Family members treat each other much better when someone's watching. If only we could remember God is actually here the whole time, maybe we wouldn't need an audience.

"Claire, you're not wearing that to school," Mrs. Webber says.

Claire has combined her goth look and her J.Crew look for a confused drama-club member in two roles at once. "What's wrong with me?" She places her hand on her hip to show her mother it may not be worth the battle. The big news here isn't that Claire is dressed strangely, it's that for the first time in my memory, Mrs. Webber notices.

Claire huffs off to our room, changes into jeans and the goth half of her choice, and reemerges. "Better?"

Her mother sighs. "Fine."

It's strange being dropped off in a Lexus. I thought I'd emerge like some starlet on the red carpet (with my underpants and princess legs, of course), but no one pays us any mind. Once I thought it was the Pontiac. Now I know the truth.

Chase meets me in the hallway, and I'd like to say I know better than to be moved by his presence. But I am me.

"Daisy, how's your wrist?" he asks, and I want to tell him everything, but I stop myself and try to don a cold expression.

"It's fine. Healing very well. I'll have a scar, but—"

"About that night, Daisy, I think you have the wrong idea."

"Look, I understand that you didn't want to get in trouble, especially after the rocket fiasco, but your survivor training could have helped someone that night." I meet his eyes and look for the truth in them. "You could have helped me."

"I don't expect you to understand, but I have a mission

220

in life. I was meant to be in the Air Force, meant to fight for my country. I can't turn off my focus." He shakes his hand in the air. "Here's a fact for you. Winston Churchill had to give the order to leave the wounded behind in some cases. To win the war, he had to select the right battles."

"Winston Churchill? You're going to compare yourself running to Winston Churchill?" My mouth is hanging open. "Maybe I'd feel differently if you hadn't left *me* behind."

Amber Richardson walks toward us, her heels clicking on the floor, the steady stream of heads turning to watch the show. I'll give her one thing, that girl can enter a room.

"My dad's suing your friend's mom," she says to me. "I assume you know that."

"I assume he knows you weren't invited and came anyway?" Which isn't true but feels good to say.

"You tried to kill me at that party, and don't think I don't know it. Little Daisy May with her perfect grades and new store-bought jeans. Don't think any of us are fooled at all by the real you."

"I gotta get to class." Chase does what he does best and runs from the conflict. Amber turns to follow him, but he's gone.

"Amber," I call after her.

She flips her hair around like she's going for the perfect shot. She poses well, with her hand on her hip and her attitude in check. "My dad's hired an investigator. You won't get away with this."

"Amber, I don't know who gave you that pill, I really don't. But I know it wasn't Max since he was with me, and I know it wasn't me. I also know that Max went inside to get you when Chase didn't."

"Oh my gosh, you're, like, completely deranged, aren't

you? He doesn't want you, dork. He never did. And just because Chase was nice enough to go to your pathetic party, it
means nothing. He's not into you, all right?"

"Amber, I'm only asking you to be careful."

She holds up her palm. "Whatever. Quit stalking us, and if
you have anything more to say to me, you can save it for the
deposition." She clicks away, her heel-to-toe motion making the
mesmerizing, succinct, and steady beat of Newton's Cradle.

☙ ■ ❧

"Oh, that is bad," Gil says as he comes in late and stares
right at my bandage.

"Third-degree in the middle there. You were expecting a
Band-Aid?"

"I thought you were trying to get out of busywork." Gil
hangs his coat next to the makeshift Christmas tree with
pre-hung ornaments. "Did you tell him at the party? Or did
you set the house on fire first?"

"I didn't set the house on fire, I—Tell who? What?"

"That nerdy kid you liked. What was his name? You were
going to tell him at the party that you had feelings for him.
Remember my advice? We guys need some encouragement?"
He looks at Lindy and Kat. "Back me up here."

I blink a few times. "Chase doesn't need any encouragement. He needs a jail cell."

"Wait a minute, what?" Gil crosses his arms before punch-
ing his palm. "Did he touch you? Because if he touched you,
so help me, I'll—"

I feel the color rise to my face. "Gil, you're so sweet. But
no, he didn't touch me."

"Are you disappointed about that?"

222

Lindy drops the phone back in its cradle. "Inappropriate question," she says through her teeth.

"Lindy, can it, I want to hear this," Kat says.

"So, did you ever tell him?" Gil asks me. "Did it work? Because you know, if it didn't work for a high school crush, I need to change my tactics."

I glare at him. "You were using me as a test?"

"Not as a test, really. More of a confirmation."

"You probably should hire someone with better skills," I say. "For your survey, not this job."

"You said you were going to tell him. Remember that, Lindy?"

She rolls her eyes.

"So." Gil approaches my desk. "Did you? No, so I ask about the party. Perfectly reasonable for me to do so. You asked my advice, I gave it, and now I want to know how it turned out. Why are you staring at me like that?"

I bring the computer to life. "Quit pressuring me. I need to get to work. I only have one good typing hand."

He blows a breath through his lips in frustration. Like I want to announce my absolute failure. It's not enough that my party was a complete bust and I found out the love of my life has the truth skills of a convict. How much humiliation should I have to endure in one month's time?

"My sister's expecting you tomorrow. Don't forget your hair appointment." He sighs and leaves for his office.

Principal Walker will not let me speak as valedictorian even if I earn it (not that I stand a chance with a month missed). He also rescinded his letter of commendation for several schools. Half the money I've saved up went to restore our family's health insurance.

223

Gil's the least of my problems.

"So, Daisy, how's the prom-date search going?" Kat asks. "So this guy's a jerk, what about someone else?"

I can be myself here, and Kat and Lindy both look to me for answers. The girls know all about my pathetic search for Mr.-Right-for-one-night. "Not very well. It seems the guy I wanted to go with isn't what he seemed, Max isn't returning my calls—and yes, I've called him. Many times." I open the filing drawer. "Worst of all, Claire and me? Our names are currently synonymous with vermin at school."

"Oh, honey, men never are," Kat says. "What they seem, I mean. That's why I wanted your mother to let you date. It's a lesson best learned young."

"It doesn't matter. It was a stupid goal anyway. My parents don't want me to go, and I'm fine with that. My parents won't like anyone who's male, but I thought I could prove myself trustworthy. Unfortunately, I went out in a blaze of glory." I hold up my bandage.

"Girl, when do you have the chance to be untrustworthy?" Kat asks. "Do they know your boss has a crush on you?"

"Shh!" I say. "He does not, and no, they don't."

I do, however, think it's hilarious that my parents believe I'm staying out of trouble by being at work, when in fact my job has the overall feel of an *Intervention* episode. (Another show I watch at Claire's since we don't have cable, and if we did, that wouldn't be on the approved list.) Claire's about dying at my house with only network television and commercials to boot. Even my piped-in internet isn't quick enough for her to view the occasional YouTube, and I must hear "How do you stand this?" every thirty seconds or so.

The swinging glass door thrashes open and hits the wall.

Someone is standing in the foyer panting. I get up quickly, because somehow I know it has something to do with me. Claire's bent over at the waist, catching her breath. She waves me over.

I push Claire outside into the open-air foyer. "What is going on?" She's in full goth dress, and the spider has made its way back onto her nose. "Why are you dressed like that?"

"Oh, I'm doing a show with your dad. Forget about that for a minute. I just came from the club. I was playing tennis—"

"You went to the club dressed like that? It looks weird with your hair and salon highlights. You can't have salon highlights and a spider nose ring. What happened to J.Crew?"

"Shut up for a minute. I was hungry, so I went to the club to eat. No offense, but I couldn't eat any more of your mom's vegetable casserole. I'm glad she's lost weight and all, but anyone would lose weight eating that for dinner. Lots of fiber—well, yeah, that's because you're eating sawdust!"

"Daisy!" I hear Gil's voice. "Daisy, where are you?"

"Shoot, it's my boss. I gotta go. I already smarted off to him once today, and he's paying for my haircut tomorrow. I waited a month for the appointment."

"Chase-Doogle-is-picking-you-up-today," she says in one breath.

"Wait a minute, what did you say?"

"Daisy!"

"Just a minute, Gil!" I yell back. "Why is Chase picking me up?"

"He said there's been a misunderstanding between you two and he wants to talk. There was obviously a real drug in

Amber's system, and he totally wants you to know he didn't do it."

"There's no misunderstanding. He left Amber to die."

She rolls her eyes at me. "He didn't know Amber was up there. She took something that made her sleepy and she'd gone to rest. Amber's such a tease, who knows where she got that med? It would be just like her to frame Chase. He never knew she was there." Claire stands up straight. "Don't you see? You're giving her exactly what she wants. You're questioning Chase, not her. Come on, in all our years of knowing Amber, list one good experience we've had with her."

"Chase left before the firemen got there. Even before the cops after Angie called! He ran away like a coward."

"He's seventeen. What did you expect him to do? Find the nearest bedroom to don his cape?"

"I thought about that. Did I expect too much? I mean, we know I have issues with perfection, but we're talking immediate selfish action. Even if he were innocent of ever asking Max a thing about a pill. And what about that? Max tells me about the pill, which I've never heard of, and then the hospital says it again that night. Is that a coincidence?"

"I'm sure there's a rational explanation."

"Chase is not who I thought he was, it's as simple as that. Getting in trouble for being at a party is one thing, but if he knew Amber was upstairs and he left before he told anyone that . . . well, you do the math."

"It's your perfect thing again. You expect people to be perfect, just like your parents. No one could meet your standards."

"Possibly drugging someone to take advantage of them

226

and being perfect are a long way from one another, even for you."

"Look, I've never understood your thing for Chase Doogle. I mean, if your taste is for high-octane milk, then yes, I guess I get it, but Daisy, he's not a criminal. Would you just make up with him so we can show our faces at school again? You know, without people wanting to throw rocks at us?"

"Even if he's not a criminal, he's not a man with integrity, and he shouldn't be allowed in the Air Force, much less their prestigious academy!"

"So what are you planning to do? You're going to tell on him? Go running to the principal?"

I hate to tell her that's exactly what I have planned. If only my father will listen.

"You're just mad because Amber's dad got him in there. You didn't think he was going to go and you want him punished."

"Claire, I'm not mad he got in, I'm mad because he doesn't belong in the academy if he's not willing to fight for what's right. I need you to believe me that this isn't about revenge. He should at least be asked about that night, and he hasn't been asked any questions or owned up to his actions. No one has even considered the fact that he was there!"

"Greg's known him forever. *We've* known him forever. He just wouldn't do what you're saying. He got nervous and left the party. Big deal. You're making a federal case out of this, and we're all paying for it."

"Daisy!" Gil is at the door. "You all right?"

"I'm fine."

Gil checks around the corner and laughs at Claire's appearance. "What are you supposed to be?"

"I'm a goth chick in trouble," she says, patting her stomach.

"You kids and your drama." He pulls the door shut. "Goodbye, Claire!" he yells through the door. "I don't want to see you here again!"

"What is it with you and guys taking a fatherly role? So annoying. So Amber is there, and—"

"Amber's where?"

"At the club. Aren't you listening?" Claire sighs. "Listen because I have to pick up my dad at the airport before I come to your house." She draws in a deep breath. "Amber's got her tennis whites that barely cover her bum. What is with that girl and her need to show her cheeks? Seriously, remember her bikini this summer? I mean, leave a little to the imagination, you know?"

My heart is pounding. Claire is going to tell me Chase kissed Amber on the tennis court. I can see him dipping her and smacking his lips to hers in this throes-of-passion way, and I prepare myself for the worst. What if Amber was fine with taking the pill? If she ended up in trouble, would she even know?

He's leaving in June, I remind myself. *It's not my responsibility if Amber gets herself in trouble.* But I feel the prick of guilt. It's as though my mother's over my shoulder! It *is* my responsibility. If I could simply eliminate my distrust, it would be one thing. But I can't, so in good conscience, I have to follow through. Although I may not like Amber, what happened to her could have been disastrous, and even if she wouldn't do it for me, I want to do the right thing because that's who I am.

Claire is going on and on, but I'm barely listening. "Then Amber walks out onto the court, where I proceed to cream

228

her because if she spent more time on her backhand and less time on her backside, she might stand a chance. So after the match—"

"You already played a whole match?"

"I told you, I creamed her."

"Chase. Get back to Chase! Did he admit to anything? Is he seriously dating her now?" My throat tightens. I imagined I could keep Chase away from Amber, but can I possibly sway Amber in any direction other than toward him? It's like she has a beacon signal around her neck.

"So Chase, who I know you've been pining over since sixth grade, is golfing at the club."

Kindergarten. I've been pining since kindergarten, and I promise you, I am no longer pining. "I have not been pining. He kissed me in kindergarten, that's as far as it goes. Sure, I may have wasted some of my romantic dreams on him, but it was nothing. It's over."

"You can't have turned on him that quickly. Come on, Greg and I are going to prom."

"You and Greg are over!"

"Yeah, but we both look good and dress well, and we don't want to mess up the picture with any half-wits, so we're going together. We'll share a limo with Chase."

"Chase and who?" I ask, knowing she can't mean me since I have yet to be asked. Chase and anyone besides me is callous, isn't it? "You're not seriously going to let Chase go with Amber. She's suing your parents and you're going to share a limo with her?"

"Do you know what those things cost? It's just a ride, Daisy. Besides, I'm not here about Amber, I'm here for you. Your prom date."

"I'm not going to the prom. I'm going to help my dad emcee," I tell her. "I knew he'd get around their rules, but he agreed to let me go. As his date."

"Tell him you're pregnant, then anything else will sound tame by comparison." Claire shrugs. And in Claire's world, this would probably work.

"My parents would chain me in the basement until I reached adulthood. And we don't even have basements in California."

"What are you talking about? I get you your fantasy moment, and you're talking about basements. Come on, forget about the party. You're going to let one moment change your entire perspective? That's just weird. We've known Chase since kindergarten. You're willing to throw that all away on something you think happened?"

"I don't expect you to understand."

"I'm serious, Daisy. You should totally be kissing my feet. Chase Doogle is picking you up from this crappy job of yours. Hello? Can I at least get a thank-you? Not to mention I have to schlep all the way over here because I can't text you like a normal person—or call you for fear your perverted boss will pick up. You, Daisy, are not the easiest person to be best friends with. Do you get that?"

"I get that." My dad took away my BlackBerry soon after it was discovered in the hospital bed. I thought I should have gotten credit for enduring a house fire, a third-degree burn, and an ambulance ride and still having the phone with me, but my father disagreed.

It suddenly dawns on me that if Chase got drugs for the party, he didn't get them from Max. Which means he might have more. "Do you have any makeup?"

"It's always more with you, isn't it? Never satisfied."

"Hey!" I point my finger at her. "The spider snot-plunged into your nose doesn't exactly make you perfection as a best friend either, you know what I'm saying?"

"I don't have my makeup, only my goth stuff. You need black nail polish? Kohl eyeliner? I'm your girl, but no makeup today."

"You need to get a real job again, Claire. You wouldn't have time to dream up this kind of trouble if you worked."

She shakes with a shudder. "I have a job. It's called annoying my parents for Jesus."

"Interesting ministry."

"Totally brilliant. I gotta run. Say hi to flyboy for me." She shakes her head. "Such a dork. I will never understand your taste in guys." She's still mumbling as she makes her way back to her car. "But I better not be in that limo with Amber."

Claire squeals off without looking, and some guy honks at her as he just misses her dad's car with his newer and bigger Beamer.

"Oh my gosh, Chase is coming." I hurry back into the office, where Gil meets me.

"Something the matter, Daisy? I mean, I hate to get in the way of your social life with work and all. Especially when you're handicapped." He looks at my bandage.

"Gil, I have no social life. Is that your idea of a joke?" I'm not feeling good enough to take a ribbing. I look like heck, I don't even own tennis whites—much less have my bum hang out of them—and maybe Chase Doogle thinks of me as a charity case. Maybe he wants to go to prom, so I'll shut up about what he did, but I'm not that easily bought off.

Gil's expression softens. "A social life is overrated in high school. Get your grades and move on. Your life is just beginning, Daisy, and all these people who make your life dramatic will be gone from your memory someday."

"That's easy for you to say."

He leans against the wall and crosses his arms. "Actually, Daisy, it isn't. I work in my dad's business, and I'm still doing what everyone expects of me. You're smarter than me, kiddo. I can't wait to see all you'll accomplish."

"Don't talk to me like I'm a dumb kid. I'm hardly smarter than you, Gil."

"Stronger than me, then. You'll do the right thing, even if it costs you. Go on, get back to work. I left the ledgers on your desk to get started on. You can file later."

I wander back to my desk, where the girls are all aflutter over what's going on.

"So your boyfriend is picking you up, huh?" Kat's gravelly voice is excited. "We get to see him? What do you think he's like, Lindy? I imagine a prep because Claire thinks he's a dork."

I look out the door. "How did you—"

"That foyer echoes, don't you know this by now?" Kat asks. "I love how everyone goes out there for privacy, and we get a show. It makes life here more interesting. Come on over here, baby. You look like—" Kat stops herself before saying what would naturally come out of her mouth. She takes out her makeup bag, and I'm feeling scared. Shaking like a cartoon character, in fact. I love Kat, but the last time she took a makeup lesson I wouldn't even venture to guess.

I push her hands away. "This is not my boyfriend. This is the guy I believe drugged a girl at the party and left her for dead."

"Don't they have easy girls at your school, Daisy? In my

232

day, the guys just went with the girls who were easy. No need for drugs. Life is so complicated anymore."

"If there are easy girls, I thought this one would have been her, but the hospital said she'd been drugged with Flunitrazepam."

"With what?"

"It's a drug that makes you forget, but she wasn't hurt, apparently."

"Thank God," Lindy says.

"But it means someone might be at my Christian high school with roofies that sedate and then make you forget."

"It sounds like her daddy's problem, honey," Kat says.

"Her daddy is a senator. He's the one who killed any questioning."

Gil comes out of his office again. "Daisy, get in here!"

I run in, fearful he's killed the computer again.

"You stay out of this or you tell your father the whole truth."

"My father can't handle—"

"Daisy, I mean it. You tell him or I will. I may not agree with him on everything, but he needs to know this." He points to the door. "Now go, and shut the door behind you."

I stumble out of Gil's office. Kat is there to greet me with her makeup bag. "My dad won't let me wear makeup, and I've got to get started on these ledgers for Gil. Thanks for the offer, though."

"Your dad won't let boys pick you up either. Do you think we're deaf?" Kat asks. "Come on, I'm sure this is all your imagination, and you want to look pretty for Chase, don't you?"

"I was sorta hoping—"

"Get over here." She smacks her desk with her transparent neon pink makeup bag. *Be afraid. Be very afraid.* Kat looks like a linebacker, so I'm not going to argue, but I'm sincerely worried that I'm going to meet Chase Doogle looking like a drag queen. And worse yet, I'll meet my father looking like some fiendish, Camaro-driving party girl from his high school days. If I want to get to the truth, I have to move Chase slowly, eloquently, seductively.

"Don't make me look like Tara Reid." This is the closest I come to an objection. "My father will kill me. Subtle. Can you do subtle?"

"I was born subtle," she croaks. "Your father is going to kill you anyway when you come home with one of these prep kids driving a foreign sports car." She points eyeliner at me. "Look up."

"A Camry," I say, blinking desperately. "He drives an old Camry."

"Hold still, for goodness' sake. I'm trying to give you a makeover."

"I've got my stuff," Lindy says. "All natural. None of it is tested on animals like that garbage Kat's using."

"It's not tested on animals, Lindy. What use does a rat have for eyeliner anyway?"

"That's not what that means." Lindy holds up her hand. "Truce! Let's get back to work, all of us. Her makeover is tomorrow with Gil's sister, not on company time."

I've had enough of the girls' bickering, and I get to work on the ledgers, looking for a respite from the backbiting.

A while later I walk into Gil's office. "I finished. I'll start inputting everything into the computer on Monday night, and then you won't have to add this up anymore. Excel will do it for you." I put the files on his desk. "The numbers look good, Gil. You've really done a good job with the business since you've come. You'd forgotten to enter a few contract numbers, so I took the liberty—"

"I can't believe you're still in high school. If I could clone you, this business would be a rousing success."

A car drives up outside and kills its lights. "He's here," I say shakily. My stomach flips. "Gil, let me practice on you. Do I look interested?" I gaze at him from the side, sucking in my cheeks.

"You look jaundiced. Just go be yourself."

I have to maintain my cool because it's dark outside, which means I am lit up like a Christmas tree in here and I have no idea what Chase might be thinking. Maybe he's thinking how sad it is that I have to work every day. Maybe he's thinking that it's a total waste of his time to have to pick me up. And maybe . . . I gnaw on my lower lip. Just maybe he's thinking, *Wow, she looks completely hot, and what a coup that I get to pick her up from work today.*

"Daisy," Gil says.

"Yeah," I say absently.

Gil whispers, "Go wash that eyeliner off. You look like a raccoon."

I run to the bathroom and look in the mirror. I look like someone who died in a horror movie, and I can't believe Gil is the only one who said anything to me. Traitors.

Chase is waiting in the lobby when I get back. He's got a bunch of red roses pressed tightly together, woven to look like the most money spent. He stands up and smiles when I come in the door. My stomach flips. I can't tell you how long I've waited for this moment. For Chase Doogle to notice me, to hand me flowers . . . and now I have to wonder if it's all an elaborate scheme to protect his future.

"Hi, Daisy," he says softly. "I know you're mad at me, but this is crazy. We have to get past this." He puts his hand on his heart. "I am so sorry that I left. I simply wasn't thinking. I know it's been really hard on you."

Before I get lost in those hazel eyes, I force myself to ask the question. "Did you try to buy a pill off of Max?" I place the flowers on the table. "Tell me the truth."

He doesn't look me in the eye, and I think of the fact that liars look to their left. Chase fidgets and wipes his mouth. A couple times. His nervousness makes me tense.

"I can't believe you'd even ask me that, Daisy! It's ridiculous and you know it's ridiculous! There's a reason that guy isn't at our school anymore. If he didn't have something to hide from, where is he? I'm back. I owned up to my mistake, and I'm going to the Air Force Academy. I did not even know Amber was in Claire's room."

My heart jumps. "I never said Amber was in Claire's room."

"You did. You totally did. You said that night, 'Run up and get her, she's in Claire's room sleeping.' You were so stressed, and see, now you can't remember anything. You were in shock."

"I wasn't in shock," I tell him. "That night I thought *Claire* was in her room, but she wasn't. Somehow you knew that, didn't you?"

Chase's face is getting red, and I want to stop myself. I want to go back to the way things were, where we forget all about my ridiculous accusations and he's just Chase Doogle, prom date of my dreams. But something won't let me drop it, and my mouth keeps talking, keeps accusing as though it's got a mind of its own.

"You knew Claire wasn't in her room, didn't you?" The way he looks at me, with such venom that I don't remember the "truth" according to him, scares me. It's as if there's something else altogether dwelling inside that perfect form I've loved since childhood. "What happened to you, Chase?"

"Me?" He slaps his chest. "Yes, it's me. You're the one having the Nancy Drew fantasies about something that never happened, and it's me who has the problem." He shakes his head. "All my friends tried to tell me about you. They said I was out of your league, but you know what? I stood up for you. I said, 'No, guys, Daisy is cool,' and this is what I get for my trouble. Accused of knowing where your friend what's-her-name was all night."

"But you did know," I say quietly.

"I don't have to take this!" He picks up the flowers and throws them at my feet, and they scatter into hundreds of red petals dotted with sprays of baby's breath. "I came here to ask you to prom because that's what I thought you wanted. I came here to make peace, but you can't let it go. You won't be happy until you save the reputation of your slutty friend. That's what this is all about, isn't it?" He snorts in disgust. "Find yourself your own ride home. And I'm not taking you to any prom or—I'm not taking you anywhere!" He runs out the door, leaving the roses on the floor.

Gil comes out of his office and stretches out his arms. "I heard everything," he says, and I let him hug me, thankful for the backup.

I have myself an ugly cry and use the back of my shirt

sleeve to wipe my nose. Gil pats me on the back and just lets me snort it all out.

"He's a liar, Daisy. It's one of my best tricks, getting the girl to think she's crazy, and I've used it way too often. I'm learning a lot here. It's a real eye-opener."

I squint at him as I pull away. "Good, because it sounds like you need to. I'm glad my pain benefits you."

He chuckles. "Come on." He puts my sweater over my shoulders. "I'll give you a ride home."

"I think my dad would appreciate that," I say.

❧ 19 ❧

Saturday morning, I awake at peace. My hand still aches at times, but the day of my vanity has arrived. Los Gatos is the kind of town where the men wear Italian shoes and silky slacks that hang as though there is money sewn in the cuffs, and on occasion they carry a "man bag," known to the rest of us as a guy's purse. I can't get past the idea of a man with a handbag. I get that it's European, but somehow it doesn't translate.

I've waited a month for a Saturday appointment. I wanted to make the most of this day and my makeover, and that took a bit of understanding of the new me. Gil's sister even offered to come in on Sunday. Sunday in Los Gatos has the frenetic energy of a puppy after breakfast. Everyone turns into Al Gore for the event, with an unstated competition of who is greener. People show up on their bicycles, carrying their cloth bags and shopping for vegetables in the sunlight. Others stroll with their designer dogs and hang out in their yoga wear while sipping nonfat soy lattes. It's a bit like my high school with better clothes and cars.

On Saturdays, however, Los Gatos is only foreign in that way where the high-end shops are too pricey for me to shop in, and the all-glass Apple Computer boutique tells me by its exterior that I cannot afford anything inside. I drive a battered, domestic car, and everyone dresses better than me here. That's the kind of world I'm used to.

As I park my father's Pontiac on the street in front of a Japanese restaurant, I worry that it will be towed simply for the crime of being a Pontiac. I don't set the alarm for obvious reasons as I prepare for my hair appointment. I have reservations about being a charity case, but the hope of redefining myself is too great.

As I enter Leighton, Chelsea's shop, there's the trickle of a waterfall and New Age music playing. I immediately want a nap since I was up late last night.

A girl about my age greets me. "Good morning, welcome to Leighton." She reaches out her hands, and I'm unsure of what to do with my own, so I keep them plastered on my handbag handles. "May I get you a cappuccino or a glass of wine?"

"Um, no. No thank you." I stiffen, immediately aware of how I don't fit into this pampered world. "I'm Daisy. I'm here for my ten o'clock appointment with Chelsea." I don't sit down, just stand nervously until a tall blonde in clicking heels comes around the waterfall and smiles broadly at me.

"Daisy!" Chelsea is taller than me, and she's wearing a gorgeous pair of black slacks with a white shirt and fitted black vest that elongates her perfect figure. "Oh my goodness, you are so cute! I mean, my brother told me you were cute, but you are darling! Maybe he didn't want to go overboard so I had to yell at him. Look at that skinny little frame. Do you model? I have someone who could do your book, if you're interested. With legs like that, well . . ."

The only things that look remotely model-like on me are

my gorilla arms and flat chest. I'm the kind of girl designers would love because I'm little more than a wire hanger, but I appreciate her gesture anyway.

"I'm just here for a haircut."

"And those cheekbones! I'm going to have a field day with you. Gil didn't tell me I was getting such a blank canvas. Don't you wear makeup?"

"I prefer au naturel," I lie. As if there's anyone on earth who doesn't mind highlighting her bad complexion. I may like the feel of no makeup, but I definitely do not like the spotted-leopard look I've been known to sport on my face. As if there's something more we girls need to make these years feel darker, we have to have acne on top of it all. When I get to heaven, I am definitely having a chat about that one.

"Even nature loves some help. I have some great tinted sunscreen I'm going to try on you. You'll be fabulous!"

"I don't want to take advantage of Gil."

"Oh, take advantage of him. Think of it as payback for the female race. It's not like you're asking him to pay for implants, right?"

"Do it, sweetheart!" A redhead bursting out of her black knit top nods at me.

Chelsea whispers in my ear, "She dated my brother for a while." She pulls back and flips her hair, her blonde tresses floating as though she's on the beach and time is standing still. Without thinking about it, I try this move and bang my head on the hard-wire brush in Chelsea's hand.

"Oooh, are you okay? I'm so sorry."

I hold up my good hand. "No, no. It was me."

"So what are we going to do today?" She runs her long, slender fingers through my hair and flips it up a few times.

241

"You've got great body, so I think we need something swingy so you have lots of movement."

"Can I have movement like your hair?"

"You have better hair than me."

"I don't."

Chelsea bends down and puts her face next to mine in the mirror. I look out the window and see Gil's blue Porsche park along the curb. "Looks like Gil's here."

"He probably wants to see what I'm going to charge him." She laughs. "Come on, let's go get you washed up."

Chelsea takes me back to the sinks, and someone else comes in to take over. "My name is Jenny, I'll be washing your hair today. What type of pressure do you prefer?"

"I didn't know there was a choice." I shrug under the wrapping of towels. "Clean pressure?"

She laughs. "Lay back." After a head massage, I am limp like a wet noodle when I walk back out to the main room of the shop. I stop abruptly and pull the towel off of my head.

"Dad!" I look at my father, who is standing next to Gil. "What are you doing here? How'd you get here? I have your car."

"Gil brought me."

"Gil?" I look at my boss.

"He came to talk to me this morning about Chase Doogle."

"I'm confused."

"I know about the party. Your mother believes I'm much more infirm than I am. My only child doesn't come home one night, I'm going to notice. I love your mother so much, honey. I haven't been the best provider, I understand that, but look at my girls. They take care of themselves so well."

"Why are you here, Dad?"

"Last night, Claire helped me out with a show. You should have seen her. You would have been so proud. That girl has a lot of talent."

"Drama's her specialty," I say.

"She told me she sent Chase to pick you up and what happened between you, but Mom told me Gil brought you home."

"He called to read me the riot act," Gil says, holding up his hands. "But I told him I'd never threaten my best employee."

"You accused Chase of something terrible," Dad says.

I fiddle with my hands.

"Do you believe it's true?"

"I do, Dad. But I don't want his whole future destroyed. But then I think, what if he's really capable of these kinds of things? Does he belong in a place that trusts him with a multimillion-dollar jet?"

"I'm more concerned that I can't trust him with one of our daughters, and that's worth far more to us dads whether we're senators or partially employed actors. Get your hair done. We have an appointment this afternoon with Principal Walker."

"You believe me?" I force myself to hold back the tears. I can see it in my father's eyes. "You trust me?"

"Always. It was myself I didn't trust. I didn't want you to make the same mistakes." He laughs. "And you didn't. You made some bigger ones. In all my years of rabble-rousing, I honestly never burned anything down."

"Can I have my 'CrackBerry' back?"

He grins. "Don't push it."

❧ 20 ❧

Prom Journal
February 3
30 Days until Prom
Fact: For every door God closes, a window opens . . . but it might be painted shut and you might be better off just staying put.

All freshened up and nowhere to go. Gil's sister made me look as good as I can, but it wasn't enough to send me into the world where I have a date to the prom. But somehow it hardly matters.

Prom is an ideal. It's not real. In my new, godlier state, I know this. I was searching for an ideal, and maybe I missed noticing some reality in the process. I imagined that if I had the perfect photo opportunity, my memories of high school would be fabulous, they'd float to the sky like a helium balloon, and my whole future would be reframed.

244

In fact, my dad's right. Ugh! It kills me to say that! But I am no worse off having failed miserably as a popular, high school party hostess. Or even as a dateless wonder on prom day. There are worse things than being dateless. I could have gone to prom with Chase and questioned all night if I could really trust him. It's nice to have my dad as an excuse. I don't date. That's why I'm not going to prom.

I mean, let's say I am right about Chase—that he does have some tendencies toward the deviant, scary, and downright perverse. Let's just say there's an 8 percent chance—heck, a 2 percent chance. I'm better off to realize it now, before anything might happen. Maybe God knows I wasn't strong enough to ward off his charms by myself, forget adding pharmaceuticals to the equation. If that's true, then my dad's prayers and freakish worry are a good thing. I've learned if I can make my dad's life more comfortable so he won't worry, maybe that's all God wanted from me.

But I'd be lying if I said I still don't think I could handle a prom date. Sure, I got burned the last time I ventured outside my box (third-degree in one place!), but as Christians, we press on, right? Toward the goal and the hope and all that. Thirty days is not impossible for God. It is impossible for Daisy Crispin, as evidenced by the previous six thirty-day periods.

Life does look different to me when I look back on the last six months, so that's something in terms of perspective. I always thought that Claire had it made. Her mother was elegant and knew the right things to say, the correct gift to bring for the occasion, and the right people to stand next to in the society pictures, but that was only on the surface. Underneath, her mother was broken, and her parents' marriage nothing more than a mirage.

Their house partially burning down was a blessing. No, really. Practically everyone whose kid was at the party sued them for child endangerment, neglect, personal suffering, and worse. (Apparently that verse about Christians not suing one another is valid only in certain states.) Claire's dad's back home and going into litigation again, rather than teaching like he's been doing. I imagine it's going to be a full-time job to keep what they have left. Mrs. Webber took control of the insurance, the rebuilding of the left side of the house, and the attempt to piece together what Claire and I destroyed in one night.

Financially they'll probably end up with practically nothing. But emotionally? Her family is whole for the first time. Claire's parents came back to lean on one another. Since everyone else abandoned them, they didn't really have a choice. They came to lean on Jesus, faith, and each other—since there wasn't a lot of anything else left.

So it's all about perspective. Burning down the house—

not such a great idea, but refining the Webbers through heat? That was a beautiful thing. And when I look at the blank page in my scrapbook marked "prom," someday that will be a beautiful thing too.

Claire's dad is working for a pharmaceutical company as in-house counsel, and her mother is—get this—helping my mother piece together dorky aprons. The kind she might have donned herself a few months ago, for a catered party.

For me? I learned that not only is perfection a myth, it can't be created. Only God knows your perfect life, your perfect mate, your perfect future. We only get part of the story.

So I'm burning my prom journal, and with it, my idea of perfection. The fact is, my perfect prom date is not even mentioned in this prom journal. Until now.

Max Diaz

Max Diaz

Max Diaz

He's not taller than me. He's not Chase. He's not even on my list. Worst of all, he wants to be a pastor, which is exactly what my father wanted for me. I am still shuddering over the thought. That is not even funny.

I blew it with Max Diaz. My image of perfection clouded God's vision, and I learned a hard lesson. I left Max out pacing the porch while I went to a party to chase after a guy . . . well, a guy who clearly wasn't worth the

Chase. I lost the affection of someone who truly mattered. Someone willing to rush into a burning building and save a complete stranger. Even if he'd known Amber Richardson, I think he still would have gone in after her.

So goodbye, prom journal. Goodbye to the idea of perfection. May you never rear your ugly head around here again.

I throw the journal into the fireplace and watch it catch. The flames lick at its edges and take to the frilly parts first. My father comes up behind me, stares in the fireplace, and puts his arms around me. I startle at his touch.

"I'm proud of you."

"I thought you'd worry I was starting fires again."

"You're putting them out, Daisy. That's what I like to see." He squeezes my shoulders. "God has something better for you. Whenever one door burns down, a window opens." He laughs in his jovial way. It's a laugh I remember well, and one far too rare for the last few years.

❧ 21 ❧

P-day—March 5. Prom is here. My date is not.

The day of prom is like the day before. I thought I'd feel differently.

I put Kim Walker on my iTunes, and her voice takes me away, floating into worship. Her voice is so pure, she reminds me that life's upsets have nothing to do with the purity of the way God loves me. I'm dateless. So what?

My bottom lip quivers, and my daddy takes me in his arms. "It's all right, sweetheart."

I nod. "No, I know. It is."

He lifts up my chin. "I've found in my years, whenever life looks this dark? God has a surprise as bright as lightning in your future."

"What if he doesn't?"

"It just means you have to wait longer, that's all. He's faithful."

I nod again, biting my quivering lip.

"You should go get dressed. I told Principal Walker we'd be there by eight thirty."

"Dad?"

"Yes, Daisy?"

"I'm glad you're here. I mean, I'm glad you went with me to talk to Principal Walker. Even if he didn't believe me."

"You did the right thing, Daisy. Let it go."

"He's just making us an example, Dad. All of those kids were at the party, yet we're the ones working at the prom? Poor Claire thought she and Greg would be going. And Greg set his field on fire!"

My dad's sympathetic but unmoved. "Principal Walker does not want to teach this lesson again. Anything could have happened that night."

"I'm good that there's penance to do. We burned half Claire's house down and turned our fake *Gossip Girl* soiree into a kegger. Not exactly setting the bar high at the Christian high school, I get it, but it's been three months." I hold up my wrist. "I have a reminder every day." I turn on the lamp in the waning light. "Do you think he enjoys this, Dad?"

"Who?"

"Principal Walker. He took away my valedictorian speech. He refused to believe anything about Chase being at the party, and now he's having us all work like common scullery maids at the prom. Do you think he enjoys it?"

"I don't think so." My dad is wearing a proper black tux that he rented for the evening, and my mother is glistening in a red silk dress, cut to fit her new, slender figure. Honestly, if I didn't know any better, I'd think they were someone else's parents. Their exterior is nothing next to the beauty within. They believed me, and I am forever changed by that knowledge.

"We're dressed pretty well for being common scullery maids." Mom laughs.

Dad tugs at his cuffs. "I wouldn't say Principal Walker

enjoys punishing you. People do strange things out of fear. He fears if he lets up on you at all, other kids will try these stunts and he'll lose control." He stops fiddling with his suit and looks at me, putting his hands on my cheeks. "It's the reason I watched you so closely, sweetheart. I was afraid, but God doesn't give us a spirit of fear." He gazes at my mother and smiles at me. "It's when I worried that I really might have lost you, that's when I learned what real fear is. It's like your mother trying to protect you from the truth about my health. But we learned that everything else, even my daughter burning down a friend's house, is survivable. Fear doesn't change a thing."

Mrs. Webber comes out of the guest bedroom wearing a white organza dress with a side of ruched ruffles on the left. It seems so strange to see such a vision of classic elegance emerge from our tacky, baby blue bathroom. The months in our home have taken their toll on her once flawless beauty, and her smile is clipped. "Are we ready?"

"You look beautiful," I tell her.

She pushes my hair back. "You're sweet, Daisy. You'd better get dressed. It's nearly time to go."

"I'm wearing what I'm going to wear." I look to the clock, then down at my peasant blouse and jeans. "No sense wasting a dress on working. It's not as though I'm going to fit in." But as I look around me, I see I'm the only one who feels that way. My mom opens the hall closet and pulls out my dress, the beautiful flamingo organza gown with the Victorian clip.

I rush to the closet. "What happened? Did you find another one?" I clutch it to my cheek and brush it against me like a baby blanket. "Oh my goodness, like buttah! Mom, where did you find it? Did you get it at Goodwill?"

"Goodwill? Find another one?" Mrs. Webber laughs. "Your mother made that! She took the clip off the old one, of course, but that's a better dress. The stitching is practically couture. Your mother is incredible."

"It's well-constructed," Mom says humbly. She leans into my ear and whispers, "I sewed in a little padding. You know, up top." I run into my room, slip into the dress, and look at my reflection in the mirror. I let the light fabric twirl, and it clings in its swingy, feminine way. I pat the spongy chest my mother stitched in, and I grin. She gets it. She finally gets it.

My reflection fills me with melancholy. There's something so lonely about looking your best and knowing there's no one at the other end to care. "This is it," I tell the mirror. "The night I waited for all year."

I emerge from my room to find everyone waiting for me. "The car's here," my dad says.

"The car?"

"Mr. Webber rented us a limousine. We're going in style." My father hooks elbows with my mother and me and allows Claire and Mrs. Webber to exit the house first.

"You've grown up a lot this year," my mom says. "I'm so proud of you, sweetheart."

∮ ▪ ∯

Walking into prom with my parents is the ultimate in humiliation. At least I thought so until Principal Walker greets us at the top of the stairs. "Well, I do hope you won't make me regret allowing parents to chaperone tonight." He winks. "Claire and Daisy, why don't you come with me? I've got the perfect job for you two." He holds out two handheld instruments. "These are Breathalyzers. Your job this evening will

252

be to make certain everyone coming up the stairs and gaining entry into our prom is perfectly sober, and then they'll walk to the next station, where security will inspect their handbags and camera sacks."

I grab the small black device. "I don't know how to use this," I tell him.

"Clearly." He holds it up. "Breathe into it like this."

Claire pipes up. "I cannot believe I'm here. No date, my dad present, now I'm testing people's stinky breath? When's the punishment going to end?"

Mr. Webber stands beside her. "Claire, what did we talk about?"

"But I didn't know I'd be doing this. What about swine flu? SARS? Is this safe? Can you make us do this?"

Mrs. Webber gives her a dirty look. We both take our stations behind the makeshift entry table draped in our school colors of blue and gold. Our parents leave us to attend to the dance floor; their job is to ensure there is no grinding or inappropriate dancing. If there was ever a job custom-made for my father, there it is.

Greeting my peers with a Breathalyzer in their face is akin to giving them the opportunity to pummel and abuse me. It's like a hall pass.

I'm fine for a while, giggling with Claire about certain dresses, until Chase appears next to Amber Richardson. She's wearing an aqua princess gown with sparkles and a full skirt. Somehow my punishment was fine until seeing Amber and Chase. It seems their sin was no different from mine. They were at the party. Amber was where she didn't belong, and yet I'm here with a Breathalyzer and she looks like Cinderella.

"Does Cinderella rent her dress out?" Claire asks Amber. "Did you get the glass slippers? Or were they extra?"

"Very funny." She smirks. "I suppose if I couldn't get a date, I would have spent more money on my dress too."

They pass their tests and we push them on. I spin around and watch them go. "Good riddance to them both."

"You all right?"

"I'm fine. As long as he's not really dangerous, it's fine. All I can do is pray about it. I'm not perfect, but neither is he. I suppose I made Chase up in my mind—for the most part."

"You girls are done," Principal Walker says as he walks over. "Claire, you'll be working with your mother in the photo booth, and Daisy, you're in the ballroom with your parents, chaperoning the dance."

"Whoopee!" I say, spinning my finger.

"It's that kind of attitude that put you here in the first place."

The ballroom centers around the parquet dance floor. Round white café tables with gold and white balloon arrangements hug the floor's edges. As I walk through the crowd, I hear my name often.

"Daisy!"

"Way to go, Daisy."

Kim Fisher, a brilliant math mind and pom-pom girl, smiles in her puffy baby-doll skirt. "We know what you did, Daisy," she yells over the blaring music.

"Me?"

"Turning off the gas. Your father told everyone."

I look at my father, who is dancing like a spastic panda with my mother.

"I didn't . . . I—"

"I turned off the gas." Chase comes up behind me and whispers in my ear.

I blink rapidly. "Why didn't you say anything?"

"You thought I was drugging girls, remember?"

"I saw you come out of the house. You didn't have time to turn off the gas."

"But you didn't see me turn it off, did you? It was on the right side of the house, near the garage. Go check it if you don't believe me. Before I took off, I turned the handle. It didn't take but a second."

"I'm so—"

"Don't bother, Daisy. If you don't know me better than that, you never will."

"You let Max—"

"I tried to protect my future. I've put a lot into this, Daisy. Maybe it wasn't the best choice I've made, but you know I had my reasons." He stalks off toward Amber, and I feel as invisible as I've always felt at this school. It doesn't matter who is right. It never did. Chase and Amber are popular and therefore right, and I'm not.

I walk toward my father and "grind patrol." He and my mother could use a little chaperoning themselves. Ick.

"Daisy?"

I spin around so quickly, I lose my strappy silver sandal. "Max!" I'm breathless.

"Diaz, get lost before I call the cops." Chase is behind me again.

Max holds up his iPhone, which has a picture of Chase at the party that night, a wall of flames behind him. "Go ahead, call them. I can prove you were in that house."

"That's Photoshopped!"

255

Max puts the phone back in his jacket pocket. He takes me in his arms and whisks me off to the dance floor. I feel like a feather in his embrace, my heart lighter than air. "You're here!"

"The photographer Claire hired, he was my cousin."

"So not Photoshopped?"

"Not Photoshopped." He stops dancing and pulls out his phone again. "He also managed to catch this."

I feel as if I could fly. "It's you and me on the porch. The only good memory I have from that party."

"We're dancing the tango," he says. "Look at the determination on your face. You're ready to tango."

I giggle. "I am ready to tango."

He nods toward my father as the music stops. "Then come with me."

I pull against him. "No, what are you doing?"

"Show me you're not perfect, *Bellissima*. Tango in front of all these witnesses. Do it poorly, but state your claim."

"Oh, I'm not perfect, Max. If that party proved anything, it's that I am so far from perfect, it's not even funny."

"Prove it to me, then." He leads me to the dance floor with his arm outstretched, and I am lost in his eyes, which seem to see inside of me. "I looked at this photo for months, wondering if you could have been acting, playing me to win Chase's affections, but I saw such raw honesty in your eyes. I couldn't believe it of you. You didn't have it in you to deceive me, Daisy."

"I didn't." I take the rose from my bodice, unpin it, and grab Max's lapel in my hands while he circles his arms around my waist. I slide the pin through his jacket. "Consider this staking my claim."

The band launches into the familiar tango, and Max pulls

me up on stage. I hear the crowd cheering for us below, and I start to look, but he launches into the dance of his native land, and I never allow myself to watch anyone but Max. I turn toward the crowd, but he pushes my chin and attention back toward him.

"Will you watch them? Or live your life?"

I practice the swinging leg move he taught me and hear the students whistle. I even hear my dad yell, "Go, Daisy!"

I never see anyone but Max. His guidance is sure and my heart is pure, not cluttered by things that don't matter. "Bible college," I tell him when his forehead is pressed against mine. "I've been rethinking it."

"You'd make a perfect pastor's wife."

"You know, I've heard that somewhere before."

He touches the purity ring my father gave me. "I looked at that photograph again and again, and dreamed of this ring and the day it would be mine. With all the t's crossed, of course."

I have no idea what my tango looked like, I only know the night was truly perfect.

Acknowledgments

A book is a compilation of so many people's efforts. Since I first met editor Lonnie Hull DuPont (in the late nineties at the Mount Hermon Writers Conference), I have wanted to work with her. Our schedules both finally meshed, and this book is the result.

Working with Lonnie and her team was as great as I knew it would be. Twila Bennett, thank you for the beautiful cover choices and the thought behind the art. Janelle Mahlmann, thank you for keeping me on track and ahead of the game plan. Jessica Miles, you went above and beyond the call of duty with your galley fixes. You are all fabulous to work with, and I consider it an honor.

And finally, to my agent, Lee Hough, for putting up with my loud, rushed cell phone calls from soccer game bleachers and whirring coffee shop lines—and anywhere else you happened to catch me during my kids' hectic schedule. Your flexibility is most appreciated.

Kristin Billerbeck is the bestselling author of several novels, including *What a Girl Wants*. A Christy Award finalist and two-time winner of the American Christian Fiction Writers Book of the Year, Billerbeck has appeared on *The Today Show* and has been featured in the *New York Times*. She lives with her family in northern California.

Skylar Hoyt is the girl who seems to have it all, but the world as she knows it is beginning to fall apart.

Learn more about the Reinvention of Skylar Hoyt series and meet Stephanie Morrill at www.stephaniemorrill.com.

Girls know all about keeping secrets,
but Sophie's is a really big one.

Visit Melody Carlson at www.melodycarlson.com.

Aster Flynn Wants a Life of Her Own . . .

But will her family get in her way?

Become the Woman God Created You to Be

When you become a God Girl, your life will never be the same.

Available wherever books are sold.